AN AFFINITY FOR MURDER.

"A witty, stylishly written mystery that weaves an entertaining tale of art theft and murder which evokes the grandeur of Lake George. A marvelous debut."
—Matt Witten, Supervising Producer for CW Show SUPERNATURAL.

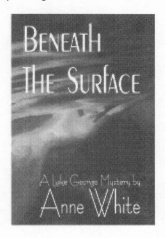

BENEATH THE SURFACE

"A charming mystery, full of twists, with entertaining characters. The residents of sleepy little Emerald Point on the shores of Lake George have some surprising secrets.
And so does the lake itself."
—Matt Witten, Supervising Producer for CW Show SUPERNATURAL

"The serenity of the Lake George resort town, which Anne White captures so perfectly, makes the quest for a girl's killer all the more urgent.
BENEATH THE SURFACE churns with suspense."
—S. W. Hubbard, Author of TAKE THE BAIT, SWALLOW THE HOOK and BLOOD KNOT.

"BENEATH THE SURFACE feeds my appetite for codes, puzzles and manipulating letters. White's cryptology, like her writing is right on."
—Verna Suit, Crossword Constructor.

"Anne White's novel BENEATH THE SURFACE immerses the reader in the chilly depths of resort-town politics, where deadly sharks glide beneath the sunny waves of tourists and attack at the first hint of blood."
—M. E. Kemp, Author of MURDER, MATHER AND MAYHEM and DEATH OF A DUTCH UNCLE.

BENEATH THE SURFACE is an engaging read that kept me captivated from the first page to the last…a compelling read with twists and turns that is hard to put down…the cover really made a great impression with me, leaving me with a slight bone chill. Bravo to Ms. White for an extraordinary tale."
—Cherokee. Reviewer. COFFEE TIME ROMANCE.

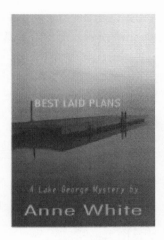

BEST LAID PLANS

"A well-structured novel highly enjoyable. It's clear style never gets in the way of the plot and the characters are pleasant to spend time with. Most likeable of all is Loren herself who can be witty without crossing the line into terminal sweetness. Compassionate and savvy, Lake George couldn't ask for a better mayor."
— Betty Webb. Reviewer. *Mystery Scene.* No. 96, Fall 2006.

"A smart, savvy sleuth, witty dialogue, ingenious plotting and a vibrant sense of place are the ingredients in Anne White's latest stew of malice and murder on the shores of Lake George. Get ready for a feast from start to thrilling finish."
—Nancy Means Wright, Author of MAD COW NIGHTMARE, THE PEA SOUP POISONINGS.

"White's technique of using Lake George as the unifying element in her series allows readers to get to know a beautiful area of upstate New York through her polished writing. The minor players represent a cross-section of society, some well-to-do and others struggling to get by. **BEST LAID PLANS** may be White's best book so far in this well-bred series."
—Verna Suit. Reviewer. *I Love A Mystery.* May-June 2006.

SECRETS DARK AND DEEP

"Anne White's delightful mystery set around historic Lake George, is a lively puzzler worthy of Agatha Christie. Tightly plotted with more red herrings than a can of sardines, **SECRETS DARK AND DEEP** is White's best yet."
—Julia Spencer-Fleming, Edgar finalist and author of ALL MORTAL FLESH.

"Loren Graham is compassionate and savvy, likeable and witty without crossing the line into terminal cuteness. Emerald Point couldn't ask for a better mayor."
—Betty Webb, *Mystery Scene* #96, Fall 2006.

"**SECRETS DARK AND DEEP** is exceptional, so skillfully written the readers gets lost in the flow and it ends all too soon. The story moves at a fast pace, nicely building suspense until a climatic, nail-biting ending. A colorful cast of characters…A galvanizing plot that guarantees edge of the seat involvement."
— Christy Tillery French, *Midwest Book Review*

Cold Winter Nights

A Lake George Mystery

Anne White

HILLIARD HARRIS

HILLIARD HARRIS

P.O. Box 275
Boonsboro, Maryland 21713-0275

Cold Winter Nights Copyright © 2009
By Anne White.

First Edition-2009
ISBN 1-59133-298-2
978-1-59133-298-5

Book Design: S. A. Reilly
Cover Illustration © S. A. Reilly
Manufactured/Printed in the United States of America
2009

Dedication

For my children—Kate, Michael,
James, Richard, Charles and Steven

Chapter 1

All signs pointed to Emerald Point's best holiday season ever.

Of course, that was before we learned about the murder.

In mid-November, almost a year into my second term as mayor, the local merchants, in what they called the dawn of a new era of cooperation, pulled out all the stops in a massive effort to create the best holiday season on record.

An enthusiastic committee hung sparkling new decorations on posts and wires throughout our Main Street business district and even rigged up an amplifying system to play holiday songs and announce special sales. If that wasn't enough to attract shoppers to our small downtown, the stores organized a series of special shopping nights designed to encourage locals to buy their holiday gifts in Emerald Point instead of dashing off to the malls in Queensbury and Albany to make their purchases.

Everyone got into the act. Local coffee shops and restaurants extended their hours. Mario's Pizzeria offered special pizzas for shoppers both before and after their forays into the stores. Even Mother Nature cooperated. For three nights in a row in early December, as the shoppers and pizza eaters headed home and the storekeepers tallied up some of their highest totals ever, a light snow shower swept off the lake and deposited a delicate dusting of white over streets and buildings. The town looked like a picture post card of an Alpine village.

Then, in the most amazing seasonal surprise of all, my seventeen-year-old friend Josie Donohue, a confirmed iconoclast who rarely went along with anything adults approved of, agreed to sing a solo in the town's Holiday Concert. The event, sponsored jointly by the Girl Scouts and two of our local civic groups, was scheduled to be held in our Village Building the week before Christmas. Josie's mother, Kate, once she'd recovered from her initial shock, expressed cautious approval. I, the eternal optimist, chalked Josie's decision up to the onset of maturity.

The only dark cloud in all this—if you could call it that, and I did—was the presence in the area of Kate's ex-husband and Josie's father, Tim Donohue. Tim, who hadn't been seen or heard from since shortly after his divorce from Kate fourteen years earlier, had appeared unexpectedly a few months before, rented a small mobile home in a trailer park a few miles north of town and declared his intention of making up to Josie—and to Kate too if she would let him—for his years of neglect. A declaration which sounded sincere, but was considered by most people who'd known Tim in the old days as a recipe for disaster.

The evening of the concert, Nature rolled out another perfect December night, cold but clear, with stars enough to set the dark waters of the lake glistening with reflected light. At six-thirty when I made my nightly drive through our downtown, I counted almost two dozen people wandering in and out of the stores. A huge turn-out for an Emerald Point evening.

Kate, who'd let Josie take her car for the concert, was waiting for me just inside her front door. The minute she saw me pull up, she came rushing down the walk. She was wearing what she called people clothes—meaning she'd foregone both the jeans she wore for chef duties at her coffee shop and the neat black uniform and white apron she favored for her catering gigs. For this special occasion she was decked out in a fitted rust wool coat and a bright multi-colored scarf which accented her shining dark hair and eyes and made her look more like Josie's sister than her mother. The only jarring note—the traces of worry I could see in her face.

"Was the star nervous about her performance? Are you?' I asked as she swung onto the seat next to me.

"A little, I guess. I'm more concerned about Tim turning up at the concert. I'm sure it will start tongues wagging, if they're not already."

"You don't think...?"

"That he'll be high on one thing or another? He swears those days are long gone, and I'm trying to believe him. I just don't know what to expect—tonight or any other time he's around for that matter."

"Well, you're coming to my house afterward, so we can leave as quickly as you want."

Earlier that week I'd invited Kate, Diane Anderson and some other friends, along with a few political associates, to a small gathering at my house. Don Morrison—I was trying to get used to calling him my fiancé—had agreed to arrive early and have everything ready when Kate and I returned from the concert. For once, I wasn't relying on Kate's Catering to feed my guests but had actually prepared the party fare myself. Not quite up to Kate's standards but, truth be told, I felt rather proud of myself.

The auditorium in the new community center was filling up fast when Kate and I hurried down the aisle to secure seats close to the front. We both stole a few minutes from reading our programs to check out the crowd and greet friends and neighbors. A little before eight, I saw Tim Donohue come in alone and slide quickly into a seat on the opposite side of the auditorium.

"Tim," I whispered to Kate and nodded in his direction.

"She'll be glad he's here. All these years without a father, I know it will mean a lot to her."

The lights dimmed. A boy stuck his head around a door at the side of the room, surveyed the audience, and then stepped out. A dozen other high school students, both boys and girls dressed alike in black slacks and white shirts, followed him. They moved slowly in single file and carried their instruments onto our makeshift stage, decorated tonight with strings of white lights. The six or eight girls in the group mounted the steps confidently, heads high, faces shining with pride. Most of the boys, either from shyness or reluctance to perform, shuffled along, then trudged reluctantly up the stairs as if ascending the steps to a guillotine.

The audience broke into applause as the young people took bows and found their places in the chairs set out for them on the right hand side of the stage. As soon as they'd settled in, Lynn Martino, the band and chorus director on loan from the Lake George Village schools, swung out from the wings. Lynn, her large frame enveloped in a bright green velvet caftan, made a few welcoming remarks and raised her hands to signal the opening number.

The band launched into a mix of seasonal pieces—we're careful here in Emerald Point not to offend anyone so they weren't bona fide Christmas carols—and then the chorus of boys and girls in gray slacks and navy blazers filed in and arranged themselves in three rows on the left side of the stage.

After a song or two I didn't recognize, Josie, her clothes neatly pressed, her hair curling softly around her face, stepped forward and placed herself at the microphone at the front of the chorus. Then, accompanied only by Lynn on the piano, she began to sing "The Little

Drummer Boy."

As her sweet contralto rang out clear and true in the hushed auditorium, tears scratched at my eyes and my throat tightened. This might be the nearest I'd ever come to having my own daughter, and even this seemed more than I could handle. How could this child—no, no longer a child, this young woman—dressed like the other chorus members, her dark hair tidy for once, her face serious with concentration, how could this girl who had in the years I'd known her bulldozed her way through every awkward stage in the book, plus some new ones I'd never heard of, this girl who'd driven her mother—and me too sometimes—to distraction at every opportunity, how could she suddenly look so beautiful and sound so like an angel? I didn't dare glance toward Kate for fear I'd cry in earnest.

I was gnawing on my lip and concentrating so hard at holding back my tears I didn't realize that someone was whispering to me until one of the Malcolm sisters seated next to me tapped my arm. "That man's trying to get your attention," she said, nodding toward the aisle.

Four seats away at the end of our row, Investigator Jim Thompson of the Warren County Sheriff's Department crouched in the aisle, making hissing noises in my direction. Jim didn't wear the department uniform, but at six-foot-six with his broad frame and imposing carriage, even kneeling in an aisle, he made an impressive figure.

I gave him a dirty look and shook my head.

"Yes. Now." He spit out the words and made a come-out-here motion.

I sucked in a deep breath and shook my head again.

Josie's last notes trailed off into silence. The crowd burst into applause. I nudged Kate, pointed to Jim at the end of the row and slid across the women next to me.

As soon as I moved, Jim stood up and headed for the rear of the auditorium. I ducked my head, avoided eye contact with everyone staring at me and trailed after him.

"Jim what in the world's going on?" I demanded as we reached the lobby.

He pulled open the door to a small anteroom. "In here. We can talk in here."

I followed him into a small office, used mostly for keeping track of ticket sales and counting receipts after events. He yanked out a straight chair next to the desk and motioned for me to sit. Without bothering to remove his navy top coat, he dropped down onto another chair facing me.

Now in the glare of the overhead light, I could see that he looked exhausted, his usually tidy helmet of gray hair tousled, his face drained of color, the lines around his mouth etched deep. Something serious had obviously happened, and it couldn't be anything good. Jim usually didn't get called in on a case until after it was determined a crime had been committed and the deputies had completed the initial investigation at the scene.

A dozen questions tumbled around in my brain, but I knew better than to ask them too fast. I waited, gave him time.

"You know Denise McNaughton, moved here four or five years ago?"

"Know who she is."

"Nurse. Bought the old Wilson farm up on Seneca Hill?"

"I don't know her well. Why?" I pressed my lips together, tamping down my curiosity.

"Neighbor of hers went in early this afternoon. Thought it was funny she hadn't seen any signs of life around the place since yesterday. Found her dead."

"Dead? How?"

"Brace yourself, Mayor. This isn't what you're gonna like to hear. No more than our department does. She was murdered." He stopped talking and stared at me.

"My God, how? Tell me." My head felt like it was going to explode. I wanted to reach out and shake him, but I knew he'd provide the details in his own way and his own time.

"Beaten first. Hit with a hunk of wood taken from a pile near the woodstove. Condition of the living room indicates she put up quite a fight. Somebody really wanted to make sure she was dead."

"Not just knocked out?"

"Wanted her dead, I'd say. Struck several times, it looks like, then strangled."

"She lived alone up there, didn't she? Were there signs of a break-in?"

"Hard to determine. You know how people don't lock their doors around here. Somebody could have walked right in."

"Anything missing that you can tell? Any signs of robbery?"

"No way to tell. Drawers weren't pulled out anywhere. No sign anybody searched her desk or a bookcase in the living room. No money around anywhere now."

"Drugs? She was a nurse, wasn't she? Helped out her elderly neighbors with their health problems, I've heard. Any chance she could have had drugs at the house?"

"We'll be paying close attention to that aspect of the case, of course. Also we're getting a list of patients she's cared for, anybody she's had contact with recently."

"Could you tell when she was killed?"

"No lights on. Fire in the wood stove had gone out, but it's hard to link that to the killing. She owned a dog—a big German Shepherd. It was outside, had access to a small outbuilding so maybe it slept out there. If it barked, nobody claims hearing it."

"Do you have any suspects?"

"Not right now. We'll let Doc do the autopsy, see what we get from his report, notify her relatives, talk to the woman who found her again and some of her other neighbors."

I didn't dare mention how tired he looked—Jim didn't appreciate that kind of comment—so I came as close as I could to offering sympathy. "Doesn't sound like it's going to be much of a Christmas for you. You been up there all day?"

"Yeah. And going back now. First, I'll talk to a few people here, let them spread the word. I'd like to think folks would lock up good tonight, not take any unnecessary chances."

That remark shocked me. "You think the killer might still be around?"

"Can't say. Could be long gone or could be hiding out nearby. Houses are pretty spread out on that mountain, you know. Lots of 'em have outbuildings and barns that would make good hiding places. You'd think whoever did it would want to clear out of there fast, but we can't know for sure. And of course, the killer could be somebody lives around here. You realize that, don't you?"

I didn't want to think about that, so I asked another question, one he'd given me an opening for. It wasn't a question he'd like much, but I had to know. "You say Denise's place is on Seneca Hill. What's the address, do you know off hand?"

"I get what you're asking, Mayor. The house is a mile or two beyond the town line, so it's in Mountainside. Still part of the county, but it's got its own post office. Emerald Point's off the hook."

I didn't comment, but a wave of relief swept over me. At least the murder didn't take place in our town. We've finally caught a break, I told myself. We're out of the woods on this one.

Wishful thinking.

I couldn't have been more wrong.

Chapter 2

Within minutes after Jim and I left the anteroom, the concert ended and the young performers began taking their bows to thunderous applause. I found Kate and, as we hurried down the aisle to join the throng milling around the stage to congratulate the performers, I glanced back to see Jim speaking quietly to three or four people near the exit. When I looked back a second time, he'd corralled another group and was talking to them at the side door.

If his goal had been to spread the news of Denise McNaughton's death quickly, he accomplished it. Even before I reached the stage to speak to Josie and the other youngsters, word was being passed through the crowd. I overheard snatches of conversation as people filled one another in.

Fortunately, Josie was still caught up in the concert. "Was I really all right?" she whispered as Kate and I hugged her, "I wasn't anywhere near as nervous as I thought I'd be."

"You were wonderful," we assured her. We added a dozen more accolades, then stepped back to allow a gaggle of her friends to fling themselves on her.

As Kate and I started toward the door, she touched my arm. "What did Jim want to talk to you about? People are all keyed up about something."

"Tell you in a minute. If we don't move fast, we'll never get out of here."

We hurried down the aisle and out the side door. As soon as we got in the car, I told Kate what Jim had said. "I'm sorry to spoil a wonderful evening this way, but everyone in town is going to know in an hour."

I heard Kate's quick intake of breath. "They're sure she was murdered? It couldn't have been some kind of accident?" she asked.

Exactly what I'd hoped too. "No. I asked. They're sure it was murder. No doubt about it."

She dabbed at her eyes with a tissue. "I don't believe this. Who would want to kill Denise? Everybody liked her."

Apparently someone hadn't. "That's what Jim will have to find out. I don't envy him the job. He looks exhausted already," I said.

"I don't like to think Josie and her friends are going to be out partying tonight. I wish I could tell her to go some place safe and stay there," Kate said.

"Has she got her cell phone with her? Maybe you can reach her."

Kate pulled her phone out of her pocketbook and dialed Josie's number. No answer. That wasn't alarming in itself. She probably hadn't turned it on yet but, even when she did, there were pockets all around, especially further into the mountains where cell phones didn't work.

"She probably hasn't had time to get any place yet. Try again from my house, why don't you?" I said.

Kate snapped the phone closed and dropped it back into her pocketbook. "You're right. I'm not going to be a worry-wart and spoil your party. I've been looking forward to it all week."

As we pulled into my driveway, I tried to quiet my own thoughts about the murder. A number of cars were already parked along the street and the sound of voices floated toward us as we got out of the car.

The rambling old house which had been my grandparents' home for so many years glowed with welcome. Don apparently had arrived as promised while I was at the concert, turned on the outside lights and plugged in the electric candles I'd put in all the windows upstairs and down.

A couple of weeks earlier, I'd dug out my stock of old-fashioned Christmas decorations, some of which had belonged to my grandparents, and added a few new ones I'd purchased at last year's post-holiday sales. I fastened evergreen wreaths with sparkly gold bows to the doors and draped strings of small white lights over the bushes at the side and back of the house. Following a tip from a holiday magazine, I replaced the bulb in the yard lamp with a string of little white lights clustered inside the glass and then twisted ropes of evergreen around the black metal pole. As a final touch I added a strand of sleigh bells and tied them on with a big gold bow.

Beyond the front lawn with its soft blanket of snow, the lake, visible only as an undulating dark mass, pulsed with its steady beat. Lights from the docks and windows of houses across from us outlined the opposite shore. In another month or so, after the lake had frozen, I'd see the lanterns of fishermen and the headlights of snowmobilers, making their forays onto the ice.

As Kate and I slipped into the kitchen, the clatter of conversation grew louder. A dozen guests had already arrived, and Don had started them immediately on drinks and hors d'oeuvres.

"I was beginning to worry about how long you'd be held up," he said as he rushed over to give both Kate and me a kiss. "I've heard the bad news about Denise McNaughton, so I assumed that's what kept you."

I nodded. "Jim pulled me out of the concert to tell me. I wish he'd held off, but I guess he wanted word to get around quickly so people wouldn't take unnecessary chances tonight."

Teddie Murray, the newest member of the Emerald Point Common Council, a woman famous for having the sharpest ears in town, sprang out of her chair and charged across the room to where we were talking. "You mean Jim thinks the murderer might be wandering around somewhere nearby? Does he know who did it?"

"No. Let me get my coat off. I'll tell everybody what he said. Then maybe we can put this aside for now."

The best approach, I thought, but one which proved to be wishful thinking on my part. Most of the guests, those already on hand and others as they arrived, wanted to talk about nothing but the murder. A few stopped long enough to take a breath and compliment Kate on Josie's performance, then jumped right back into questions and speculation. Even my hors d'oeuvres, which I pointed out to everyone I'd made myself, couldn't compete.

Part way through the evening, Teddie, a short, stocky fifty-year-old who relished her new role as a council member a little too much sometimes, seized my arm and pulled me aside. She puffed out her chest and furrowed her brow as she glanced up at me. "This is very serious, Loren. Maybe you and I should get together tomorrow over lunch and decide how to handle it."

"Handle it?"

She pursed her lips. "You know this isn't a good thing for the town."

"I'm not sure what you mean," I said again.

"Even if she didn't live right in Emerald Point, it's bad for the area's image."

Teddie, a single mom whose children were grown and off on their own, was the first woman elected to the council in five or more years. She seemed to have an overabundance of time on her hands and, as the third or fourth generation of her family to live in Emerald Point, rated the loyal support of a coterie of relatives and friends interrelated through marriage or jobs.

"Malcontents, all of them," Pauline had characterized the family and, from what I'd been seeing from Teddie at Council meetings, the description fit.

I shot down the lunch suggestion fast. "I've got a lot scheduled for tomorrow, Teddie. And anyway, we'll want to take our cue from Jim. We'd best wait to see what he finds out."

She was gearing up to argue that point, when, fortunately, Don signaled to me from the kitchen.

"Oh, oh. Trouble with the oven, I bet," I said and eased away.

But there was no getting away from the talk about Denise. All evening her murder dominated the conversation, her murder along with the piecing together of bits and pieces of information about her that people had gathered during the four years she'd lived at the lake. Two husbands and a couple of male friends, romantic male friends that was, scored high on the gossip meter in this part of the world.

Finally, Dave Stanton, another council member, interrupted. He banged his hand on the arm of his chair. "Let me tell you people something. She was a wonderful nurse. That's what we should be talking about. She took care of both my parents when they were in the hospital, couldn't do enough for them."

His remark finally closed off the conversation about Denise, but by that time the party was winding down and people were saying their good nights.

Teddie still wasn't ready to give up. She sidled up to me as she was zipping up her navy parka. "I still think we should plan our response to this, Loren. Give me a call, why don't you, after you hear from Jim."

Sometimes repeating oneself isn't a sign of memory loss; it's a desperation tactic. "I'm sure Jim will come up with a lot of information we don't have right now," I assured her and pushed the door gently, but firmly closed behind her.

After the other guests had filtered out, Don and I surveyed the scene. "Our first party as a bonafide couple, and we were upstaged by a murder," he said.

"Hardly worth facing all these dirty glasses and dishes for," I told him.

"You don't have to face them. I'm clear for tomorrow. You go to work and I'll have everything washed, polished and put back where it goes by the time you're through."

It was a generous offer. We'd managed to squeeze the leftover food back into the refrigerator, but dirty glasses, food-encrusted plates and half empty coffee cups covered every flat surface, and the dishwasher was already full. Cleaning up would require a lot more time and energy.

"Are you serious?" I said.

"Absolutely."

Apparently, being engaged had advantages I'd never considered. Since I was an emancipated modern woman, I didn't give him any argument.

I did, however, find ways to show my appreciation.

Chapter 3

By the time Pauline Collins, our Village Secretary, burst into the office at noon the next day—an hour before her agreed-on arrival time—I was already processing a sizeable amount of information about Denise McNaughton, her life in Mountainside and her work as a nurse at the Glens Falls Hospital 20 miles away. But I knew that no matter how much I'd gleaned from the party guests, the morning paper and the initial radio and television news reports, Pauline would be willing and able to fill in many more blanks. In fact, I was counting on it.

Five years before, when I was elected mayor of Emerald Point for the first time, I'd been more than a little apprehensive about Pauline and her role in Emerald Point government. She'd been a legacy from my predecessor, longtime mayor and beloved North Country politician, Young Ned Chamberlain. Young Ned, well into his 70's when he retired, had never outgrown either the sobriquet or his zest for life. The day of my swearing-in, he'd wished me luck and made tracks for Florida where he took up deep-sea fishing with the same enthusiasm he'd previously reserved for upstate New York politics.

Pauline, white-haired, matronly, by that time in her early sixties, had been Village Secretary and Young Ned's right arm for more years than she cared to tell, but she wasn't ready to retire simply because he'd decided to do so. Shortly after I announced my intention to run, she'd approached me to indicate her willingness to stay on the job if I hadn't earmarked someone else for the position.

"Well I have to win first, but if I do, I'd be delighted to have you," I'd said and pushed aside my misgivings about her knowing more about the job than I did.

But if Pauline was appalled by my innocence—ignorance might be the more apt description of my state at the time—she was diplomatic enough not to let on, but to steer me with careful comments like "Ned had trouble 'bout that same thing one time, as I recall, and he thought…"

And the next thing I knew, she'd thrown out a couple of possibilities for me to consider, without ever once suggesting that I hadn't come up with the solution all by myself.

The morning after we'd heard about Denise McNaughton's death, Pauline settled herself in the chair next to my desk, prepared to share any information we'd both learned about the murder.

"Reggie and I were both sorry we couldn't make your party last night," she began. "He'd signed us up to handle the phones for the rescue squad, and he isn't one to back out on something like that, especially this time of year when everybody's so busy. Our phones were ringing off the wall once word got out about Denise."

Since Pauline had introduced the subject, I jumped right in. "People must have been shocked to hear that Denise was murdered."

"They sure were. Everybody's saying what an awful thing it is. Poor Denise. Here she spent her whole life taking care of others. And now somebody's gone and killed her."

"Does anybody have any idea who might have done it?" I asked.

"Not that you'd put much stock in. Half the town—at least most of the people I talked to—think it's that Woodsman. He's been hitting places up near Tannerstown, you know."

"Wait. I thought that was two or three years ago."

"Wasn't around for a couple of years, but he seems to have turned up again. Some folks figure Denise came home from a late shift—she sometimes stayed on 'til the early morning hours, they say. In fact, when they were really short-handed at the hospital, she'd even stay over and work a double. One way or another, she came home late, and he'd gotten in and was robbing the place and he killed her."

Definitely a possibility. Everyone around the lake had heard stories about the mysterious figure people around here had nicknamed the Woodsman. He was said to live deep in the woods in one of the most inaccessible regions of Adirondacks and to take refuge occasionally during the long northern New York winters in camps and summer homes closed for the season. No one knew for sure exactly who he was or why he chose to live in the woods. Four or five years before, after he'd almost been caught, he'd disappeared completely. No one had reported any sign of him until this past fall, when rumors spread that he might be back in the area.

"But Pauline, most of the burglaries didn't involve any violence, did they?" I said.

"No, but they were at summer camps and such, closed up for the winter. Nobody staying in 'em at the time."

"But couldn't the Woodsman tell somebody was living at Denise's place?"

"Except maybe he expected her to be gone for the night. They say she left the hospital around two o'clock. That would have meant she probably didn't get home until after three o'clock. Not exactly a time he would have expected somebody to roll in," Pauline said.

I didn't like picturing what might have happened. "I suppose that could point toward him," I agreed reluctantly. "Although with all the empty summer places around, you wonder why he didn't move right into one of them instead of helping himself to what he wanted and then going back out into the woods now that it's so cold."

"Remember at least one time he did. Wasn't it Mac and Jane Rosario drove up to check on their place last spring and found he'd been sleeping in one of their beds? He'd built a fire in the woodstove and helped himself to stuff out of the freezer. They figured he'd slept there three or four nights anyway."

"Of course, he wouldn't have expected them to come back to check. Whereas with Denise living there..." I shuddered, thinking of all the times I walked into my house alone, late at night, with never a thought that someone might be there. "You said half the town thinks...What does the other half think?"

Pauline grimaced. "That somebody meant Denise harm. She's been married a couple of times, you know, and had a couple of live-ins besides. That's all it takes to set some folks off. Nobody knows much about any of her men friends, because she kept to herself up there. But there's been comin's and goin's, the neighbors say."

"Comin's and goin's?"

"Brief encounters might be a nice way of putting it."

"They aren't implying prostitution, are they? Wasn't Denise a little too old for that?" The minute the words slipped out, I wanted to call back the question for a rephrase. Denise, I suspected, had been about the same age as Pauline.

Pauline took my remark in stride and sidestepped neatly. "Anybody look as good as she did, it wouldn't matter how old she was. The woman could have passed for twenty years younger, and she had style like a fashion model besides."

"She was a great looking woman. You're right about that," I agreed.

Denise, a statuesque brunette with a terrific figure and warm, sunny smile, had always been dressed to perfection. I'd seen her dashing out of Terry's Meat Market with an armload of groceries one morning a few weeks before when she'd looked like she was heading for a party, and it wasn't even nine o'clock.

"There's a couple theories making the rounds. One is she had a new guy staying there with her and somebody else she'd been seeing came by and found out about it. Didn't like the idea he wasn't her one and only," Pauline said.

"Jim mentioned she was beaten badly. Did you hear that too?"

Pauline nodded. "Nothing much left to her face, they said, and bruises all over her body besides. Reggie talked to the guys on the rescue squad that got called in. Petey Rondeau just about fainted, they said. His first time to see somethin' like that. Not eighteen yet, I don't think."

"Poor kid," I said

"Reggie says you don't see somebody beat like that unless the killer's a nut case."

"Great. Just what we need up here. First thing I thought of was that she didn't live in Emerald Point, but we're still too close to the crime scene for my taste."

"Mine too. I'm not sure Reggie would be much good any more if he had to protect me. Not that I'd ever tell him that."

No way was I going to comment on that remark, so I said, "What else did the guys on the rescue squad say?"

"Nothing much, but Reggie's going to ask around, see what else he can find out about the husbands. One died, he thinks, and the other might have kin here in town."

Reggie, a historical re-enactor involved with a number of local organizations, laid claim—if that were possible—to even more friends and relatives than Pauline, and to as many or more sources of information.

As for people who would protect me if the need arose, I hadn't factored Don into that role yet, and I wasn't sure I planned to do that anyway. I was still getting used to thinking of him as a future husband.

But right then, I wanted to concentrate on the murder. "So now what, Pauline? I hope the sheriff's department picked up a few clues. Have you heard anything about what they found?"

"I was counting on you knowing the answer to that. Heard Jim pulled you out of the concert to give you the news. Sounds like he's got his hands full figuring out not just who killed her but why."

As if Pauline's words had conjured him up, Jim Thompson slapped his big hand hard against the office door and took a tentative step inside. "Okay if I barge in, ladies?"

"Sure. Want coffee?" I said.

"Love it."

Before I could get up, he turned to Pauline. "Maybe you'd do the honors, Pauline. No offense to anyone else here, but yours always seems to taste the best for some reason. And while you're making it, I'll run a couple of things by the Mayor."

The man was smooth, damn smooth. In less than a minute, Pauline, pleased with the compliment, had scuttled off to the reception area to start the coffee maker. Jim slid the door shut behind her and settled himself in the chair in front of my desk. He obviously wanted to talk to me privately, and he'd arranged it with ease.

"I've got a question for you, Mayor. This is strictly between the two of us. I really mean that. Understand what I'm saying?"

I nodded, trying to guess what was coming. He had all the signs of a man wrestling with a problem. Although he was freshly shaved and neatly dressed as always, his face was drained of color and his eyelids drooped heavily.

"Say you understand, please."

Since he was obviously worn out, I tamped down the inclination to snap at him. "Okay. Strictly between the two of us. Go ahead."

"Tim Donohue, Kate's ex-husband. Rented a place up in Mountainside recently. How much has she told you about him?"

I felt as if a cold hand was squeezing something inside me. I took time to think through my answer before I gave it. "Not much really. He had a drug problem, I understand. Not a great husband to Kate or father to Josie. Now he's clean and come back here, saying he wants to make up to them. Make up to Josie anyway."

"Kate gonna buy that?"

"She's on a spot, Jim. Josie wants a father. After all these years without one, you can't blame her for that. But, no. I don't think Kate's going to be too quick to believe anything he tells her."

"He staying with Kate and the girl at all?"

"Not as far as I know. Why?"

"Some indication he was friendly with the murdered woman."

I didn't want to hear what I was afraid was coming. "He didn't live very far from her, but that doesn't mean anything, does it?"

Jim set his jaw. He didn't answer. I knew that look, and I hated it. "Jim, I know there's talk about her having men friends. You're not saying Tim Donohue was one of them, are you?"

"Not saying anything right now, and don't forget—either are you."

I didn't plan to. But I knew that wouldn't stop me from worrying myself half sick about what he'd told me.

Chapter 4

As if there wasn't already enough gossip about the murder making the rounds, the next day saw the talk magnified a hundredfold.

The account in the Post Standard that morning had been limited to a couple of paragraphs on the murder and a sketchy account of the search being launched for Denise's killer. But by noon, a story about a manhunt farther north in the Adirondack Park began circulating. The minute I reached home that afternoon I switched on the radio for an update.

According to a Glens Falls station, deputies searching the area around Denise's house had found snowshoe tracks leading into the woods. Several deputies from the Warren County Sheriff's Department had followed the tracks as far as they could, but had been forced to give up at dusk. Since there'd been no new snowfall during the night to obscure the tracks, reinforcements had been brought in at daybreak to continue the search.

I lingered by the radio. The kitchen was still tidy from Don's clean-up operation two nights before, so I settled down at the table with some paperwork which had been hanging over my head.

Two hours later an announcer broke into a musical program with an update.

"We've just had word that sheriff's deputies, following those tracks they spotted last night, have been searching the woods around Arden Pond. Initial reports say they've found a structure or cabin of some kind, backed against a rock ledge. No report as to whether they found anybody in it."

An awkward pause. Dead air. Finally, he continued. "This is thick wilderness area, so searching these woods is going to take some time. We'll be bringing you updates as we get them."

At four o'clock, the unknown announcer was replaced by the

station's top evening news reporter, Billie Jorgensen. Billie had apparently been called in early to handle the story.

"That structure we've been reporting on isn't anywhere near a cabin," Billie informed his listeners. "According to the latest eyewitness reports coming in now, it's apparently nothing much more than pine boughs and tarps. At least that's the way one of the deputies described it. Hard to believe somebody lived there permanently, and we've had more than our share of zero degree weather already this winter."

Billie, a master at filling air time, recapped the search efforts and added a detailed description of the area and its remoteness. Finally, he gave up and clicked back to the regular programming.

In less than an hour he returned for an update. "As we reported earlier, sheriff's deputies aren't calling that structure they found a cabin," he explained. "They say it's not much more than a lean-to, but it appears to have been inhabited. Looks like somebody strung ropes between two trees, then hung tattered blankets on them to enclose the space. Inside there's a kind of hammock strung across between the lower branches. Could have been meant for storage space or a place to sleep. Hard to tell."

More delay. I made myself a cup of coffee and reread a report on water pollution near our town docks.

Nothing but music for a while, and not very appealing music at that.

Then Billie broke in again to relay new information. In their search of the lean-to, deputies had found several items reported stolen by area residents, some dating back to last spring. But still no sign of the person who lived there.

At six o'clock Don, arms full of groceries, pushed open the kitchen door. "I stopped at Terry's Market. The town is on tenterhooks. Everybody's got a different opinion on who this guy is and where he's disappeared to."

"You mean they really don't know who he is? I thought he'd been around the area off and on for a long time, " I said.

"Some think he's one of the Fletchers—family lived back there near Granite Mountain a long time ago. Others claim he's not the same guy was around here a few years back—he's somebody new. Nobody knows for sure, I guess."

Don unpacked the grocery bags, then washed his hands in the sink and patted out a couple of burgers. As he slipped them into the broiler, I cleared my paper work off the table and set out plates and bowls for salads.

We'd barely started our meal when Josie Donohue knocked on the kitchen door and pushed it open.

"Lor, can I come in? I need to talk to you."

The angelic choir girl had vanished, replaced by a bedraggled street urchin who would have been a shoo-in for a role as an orphan in Oliver.

"Sit down. Tell me what's wrong?" I cut my burger in two and pushed the plate with the larger piece in her direction.

"My father. People are saying they think he might have killed that Mrs. McNaughton."

"Who's saying?"

"Everybody. It's all over school. The sheriff's guys went to his house and asked him all kinds of questions—like where he was the night she was killed, stuff like that."

"But..." I started.

She shoved the plate back toward me. "I can't eat, Lor. Don't tell me it doesn't mean anything. The kids at school knew about it. Joe Roloff's father's a deputy and he told him. My father hung around at her house a lot, I guess."

"Really? You mean they were friends?"

"A heck of a lot more than friends, some of the kids been saying. The deputies didn't arrest him, but they told him not to go out of town any place. That doesn't sound good, does it?"

"No, but..." I glanced toward Don, hoping he'd come up with some reassuring remark. The coward concentrated on his burger and didn't say a word.

"So did your father tell them where he was that night?"

"Yeah. Said he was home all evening, even told 'em what he watched on television, what time he went to bed. Stuff like that."

"Isn't that all he could do? He lives alone and he doesn't have any neighbors close by. They really can't ask anyone else if he was home that night, can they?"

"Lor, I had the car that night, the night before the Christmas concert. I went up there after the rehearsal about ten o'clock to remind him about it. I even waited around a while to see if he'd come home. I wanted to be sure he remembered about my solo. That was the night Mrs. McNaughton got killed, remember?"

"You went up there that night? By yourself?"

"Sure. It wasn't that late and I wanted to make sure he came. But he wasn't home, Lor. The house was all dark and his car was gone.

20

Everything he told the deputies about being home that night was a big fat lie."

I took a bite of my burger and cast around for something which might explain her father's deceit. It wasn't easy to come up with anything. "Let's not jump to conclusions. You're sure it was that same night? Maybe he…"

She didn't give me a chance to speculate. "I'm sure it was that same night. One hundred percent. No doubt about it."

"Okay, but there can be a logical explanation." I grasped at straws, trying to come up with one. "Maybe he'd put his car in the shop for repairs. Maybe he'd already gone to bed."

"No. The garage door was open. He wouldn't have left it like that if he was home for the night. Skunks get in. Dennisons had a porcupine in their garage last year. He knows stuff like that."

"Okay. You said he told you he went to AA meetings. Maybe that's where he was, and he didn't want to say so."

"That late? They wouldn't have meetings that late, would they?" She sounded skeptical, but hopeful.

I pressed my advantage. "I think they have them at all hours. Why don't you give him the benefit of the doubt on this? No sense borrowing trouble, is there?"

I could see her weighing what I'd said. "I suppose…"

I thought of another possibility, but I saw no need to mention it to Josie. Maybe Tim was seeing another woman besides Denise and spending some of his nights with her. When he was married to Kate, he'd had a wandering foot—as folks around here termed it. One advantage of living out in the middle of nowhere was that you didn't have neighbors keeping track of what you did. Who'd know whether he spent his nights at home or not?

After Josie left that evening, Don and I did our own speculating about Tim and where he might have been the night Denise McNaughton was murdered.

"I hate thinking it, but maybe he does know something about her death one way or another," I said as we were drinking our coffee. "There's been gossip about the two of them making the rounds."

Don shook his head. "I've heard it too. The guy sure manages to get himself talked about, but that doesn't make him a murderer. And you could be right about him seeing somebody else besides Denise, maybe somebody he doesn't want to throw in."

"I suppose." I unconsciously echoed Josie's words, but I wasn't convinced.

"You know," Don said, "I don't know Tim, but he strikes me as one of those guys who never catches a break. He comes back after sixteen years or more and tries to make a fresh start. Then something like this happens."

I bristled at the remark... "Right. Comes back after Kate spent all those years alone, raised Josie by herself. She went through some really tough times, I've heard. Sorry if I can't feel one speck of sympathy for the guy."

"Okay, even if you don't, you know how this town is about gossip. Take the speculation about Denise, for example. With two unattached people living near each other, if he ran over to borrow a cup of sugar, tongues would start wagging."

I didn't see Tim Donohue as a borrow-a-cup-of-sugar kind of guy, but I let the remark go by. Sometimes I felt as if Don disagreed with me only for the sake of argument. I snatched up the coffee cups and shoved them into the dishwasher. "Let's get off this topic. There must be something else we can talk about."

We cast around for that something else, but with no luck. After we'd suffered in silence through a Law and Order rerun we both knew by heart, he reached for his jacket. "I'll go along, I guess. Doesn't seem possible tomorrow's Christmas Eve already. I'll call you in the morning."

I didn't urge him to stay. Josie's news about her father had wiped out most of my Christmas spirit—not because I cared particularly about Tim, but because of the havoc he could wreak in his daughter's life, and in Kate's. He'd stayed away for almost all Josie's young life. Why couldn't he have left it that way?

No matter who they found killed Denise, there'd be people who would always wonder if Tim Donohue was somehow involved. If he had any decent explanation of where he'd been that night, he'd be smart to get the word out fast.

The minute I opened my eyes on the morning before Christmas, I fumbled for the radio on my nightstand and switched it on. Billie Jorgensen, his voice hoarse with fatigue, was offering his listeners a recap of the news before signing off to catch what he termed some badly needed shut-eye. Billie had apparently managed to hang on all night with his trademark enthusiasm only slightly diminished.

"A search of the Woodsman's lean-to has turned up a bunch of articles stolen from area camps," Billie said, and ran through the list—"batteries, blankets, a couple of sleeping bags. They haven't found anything really valuable, like jewelry or electronic devices, but they did turn up several pairs of cross country skis, a backpack and a couple of books."

After a short pause, he cleared his throat and went on, "As many of you already know, the Woodsman eluded the deputies tracking him through most of the day, but the search ended in late afternoon just as"—dramatic pause here—"an all-encompassing darkness descended over the Adirondacks, a darkness which would surely have enabled him to escape his pursuers once again."

I wanted to get downstairs and make coffee, but Billie had me glued to the radio.

"He was finally trapped by a contingent of deputies and volunteers who'd sealed off every possible escape route. Then and only then, he surrendered quietly and was taken into custody without incident."

With that, I thought I could make a run for the shower, but Billie had even more to report.

"Strange thing about this folks," he went on, "the Woodsman had no idea why he'd been pursued, or even that his pursuers were the sheriff's deputies. He kept asking 'What did I do?' over and over, and insisting he didn't do anything as they escorted him back to a patrol car."

His questions, Billie explained, had finally goaded Lester Stohmeir, one of the deputies, into asking him, "What about those cross country skis you got on? You gonna tell us they belong to you?"

According to Lester, the Woodsman had been ready with an explanation. "Found 'em outside a barn back yonder. Didn't look to me like anybody cared much for 'em."

As Lester was gearing up to ask about other missing articles, one of the other deputies had waved him into silence. "Thompson'll be really ticked if you tip him off on the questions he's going to be asking," he'd told him. "You'll give him a chance to get his answers worked out ahead of time."

And Lester, even though he thought he was doing the right thing, had reluctantly stopped the questioning—right then anyway.

After that report which he'd apparently obtained from one of the deputies, Billie filled in with a recap of the events of the last two days, then primed his audience for his bombshell.

"There's even bigger news this morning. We can tell you now, folks, who the Woodsman is. And at this time, we're the only newscast with this information. After a lot of speculation during the night, the sheriff's department confirmed the name a few minutes ago, at 6:06 this morning to be exact. The name we've all been wondering about, the name of the man the deputies have been searching for… the Woodsman is Lucas Prendergast."

Billie paused long enough to let this sink in before he continued. "Some of the old timers here at the station remember the name. There was a good-sized Prendergast family lived up near Arden Pond some years back. We're not quite sure yet, but folks are speculating he's one of that clan. More on this as we get additional information from the sheriff's department."

I didn't need to wait for more information. I knew exactly who Billie Jorgensen was talking about. I'd known the man years before. He was called Luke Prenders in those days, but he was the same guy. I was dead certain.

I dashed to the shower and in less than five minutes I was semi-dry and reaching for my clothes. In ten more, I was dressed and downstairs. Not my best look, but good enough. I filled my travel cup with instant coffee, grabbed a cereal bar and took off for the Municipal Center.

When I arrived there a half hour later, I wasn't expecting Sheriff's Investigator Jim Thompson to welcome me with a burst of Christmas spirit, and he didn't. As I pushed open his office door in response to his bellowed "Come in," I saw that his face looked even more drawn and tired than it had the day before when he'd stopped by the Village Building.

I thought it best to start with some low-key sympathy. "You've had a long night, Jim."

"Very long. I'm not ready to discuss this case with you yet, Mayor. You've got to give us more time on this thing, before you rush in here and start asking questions."

"I know. I know." My voice dripped honey. "No questions. I only want confirmation of one thing. Luke Prenders. That's the name, right?"

Jim eyed me without answering.

"I'm anxious to see if this man is Lucas Prendergast. If he is, we go way back—friend of my grandfather's, very kind to me when I was a child."

"You may be right. But let's not jump to conclusions here. There were a good many Prendergasts in the area years ago and couple branches shortened up the name to Prenders."

"And this is Luke, Lucas, that is?" I pressed him.

"That's the name he gave us."

"Anything else?"

"Not forthcoming with much other information. We think this guy might have lived around here years ago before he moved back into the woods. Seemed to disappear for a while—at least there were no reports of him—and then we started seeing signs he was back."

"Signs?" I asked

"You know what I'm talking about, Mayor. Folks complaining about articles taken from closed up camps. Food, clothes, blankets."

"But no violent crimes, were there?" I asked.

Jim ignored my question and pulled a folder out of his top drawer. "Here's a few of the items reported stolen. Sergeant Cronin made this initial listing based on reports from people in the area. Small sums of money, food, batteries, sleeping bags and blankets. Jim Bradford's skis—he's been all bent out of shape about them. And clothes—two or three reports on work clothes taken the last couple of months."

"But stolen from seasonal homes, not from places someone was living," I said.

"No way to tell that right now. He was actually wearing articles of clothing with people's name tags sewed into them, articles they can identify."

I didn't want to hear a list. "Jim, can I see him? Talk to him a minute?"

"Not today. Why the hell do you want to do that anyway? He's probably sound asleep. He's been eating like a horse, the guys at the jail tell me. Happy with our meal plan, likes our accommodations. Now he probably wants to catch up on some shut-eye."

"He was a family friend, very close to my grandfather, around the house a lot back when I used to come up here to visit my grandparents." I hoped that much would make my case. I wasn't ready to fill him in on my most important memory of Lucas. Prendergast. He'd done me a favor once, one that meant a lot to me. I owed the guy. I owed him big time.

But a no from Jim meant no. At least until I got a chance to make it a yes.

Chapter 5

As part of her own holiday celebration, Kate Donohue invited Don and me and a few others to her house for a Christmas morning brunch.

"I would rather have made it dinner," Kate had explained when she issued the invitation, "but Tommy Davidson, the boy Josie's been seeing, has invited her to spend the afternoon and evening with him and his family, and she really wants to go. I thought it better not to make an issue of it. Do you mind?"

"Of course not. If you said she couldn't go, she'd be crushed. Plus I love your brunches."

When I'm wrong, I'm really wrong.

After a month of orchestrating one successful holiday event after another for more than a dozen of her customers, the brunch Kate put on in her own home wouldn't have rated a single star.

Don and I arrived at the suggested time—noon—to find Kate and two Emerald Point women sipping Bloody Marys and swopping details about the murder. Josie, Kate reported, was taking extra time to dress.

Kate introduced Don to her other guests, Jane Kennison and Alice Simmons, sisters I'd met several times before. They lived side by side in elegant lakeside homes north of town on what was sometimes referred to as Emerald Point's gold coast, and had become regular customers of Kate's Catering. Their husbands, both doctors with practices in Glens Falls, wouldn't be coming to Kate's brunch, they explained, because they'd been asked at the last minute to help serve Christmas dinner to parishioners at their church. Since the dinner was given by the men of the parish, the wives had been excused.

Technically present too was Diane Anderson, whose son was spending Christmas with his father. Although Diane swore she was over her divorce and prepared to enjoy Christmas on her own, she couldn't quite pull it off. Also among the missing—Tim Donohue, who'd been invited by Kate in response to numerous requests from Josie. His absence left Don in the role of only male guest.

Kate had made her reputation as a caterer by knowing how to salvage any event. She kept the drinks flowing, the hors d'oeuvres circulating, and the conversation as lively as she could make it. But despite her best efforts, nobody seemed to be in a holiday mood. The murder had cast a pall over everyone, and even the news that a suspect had been picked up and taken to the Warren County jail didn't ease the tension for some of the guests.

"I didn't sleep well at all last night," Alice Simmons complained. "Joel got called in for an accident, and I kept thinking I heard someone outside my window."

"Alice, I told you, you're making too much of this," Jane said.

"I don't think I am. I won't rest easy until they send that guy to prison where he belongs and throw away the key," Alice insisted.

"Whether he's guilty or not?" Don asked with a chuckle. He'd probably intended his remark as lighthearted teasing, but Alice didn't take it that way.

She bristled. "Everyone knows he's guilty. I can't imagine why you'd think otherwise, unless you're trying to start an argument."

"Apparently you've heard something I've missed," Don said.

His tone might have been a little sharp, but it was a long way from argumentative. He was giving her a chance to convince him.

"I've heard all the news reports. They should be enough for anyone with good sense." Alice said. No doubt in her mind, none at all.

Jane jumped in and made a half-hearted attempt to intervene, but she couldn't quite pull it off.

Before Don could fire back, I interrupted with a comment about Kate's cheese roll-ups in a desperate try to steer us toward something non-controversial. But my effort proved fruitless. Alice and Don glared at each other, both looking as if they were ready to explode.

Josie picked that moment to come bounding into the room. My first relief at seeing her disappeared quickly. With little more than a nod at the rest of us, she planted herself in front of her mother. "I don't think my father's coming. When you called him, did you act like you really wanted him to come, or did you sound like you were just going through the motions?"

Kate stared at her daughter for a minute, then side-stepped the impending argument. "Speaking of motions, I'd better make some toward the stove if we don't want to eat burned food." She jumped up and pushed past Josie to head to the kitchen.

I left Don on his own to cope with Alice and followed Kate out of the living room.

I found her leaning over the kitchen table, her face flushed. "Why did that man have to come back here? I'm sure this is just the beginning. Josie and I'll have a million arguments about him, and I'll be in the wrong no matter what I do or say."

I reached out and put my arm around her. "Josie won't be fooled for long. She's too smart for that. Just hang in there."

"I hope you're right. I shouldn't have said anything. Let's talk about something else. What did Don give you for Christmas? I know you told him you didn't want a ring but...."

"Not just told him, made him promise not to give me one. I've been down that road before. I want this time to be different."

"What then?"

I hesitated. I hated to tell her, especially now. "A membership in Triple A and a blender."

Kate's eyes widened. "I'm not sure of the appropriate response here. Help me out."

"Actually, I'm not sure myself. I may have been too insistent about keeping things casual. Give me a couple of days to think about it, and I'll tell you."

Food appeared to be the only safe topic. In five minutes I'd helped Kate cover the buffet table in the living room with an assortment of hot and cold dishes she'd prepared. As usual with Kate, her meal was fit for royalty—a perfect quiche, a platter of cold roast beef with her signature horse radish sauce on the side, three different salads, a basket of piping hot rolls.

Jane was full of compliments, asking Kate questions and commenting on almost every dish. I joined in, but the rest of the group muddled through the meal as if we were eating take-out from a greasy spoon. We all seemed to be marking time until we could announce we needed to get home.

Don stayed unusually quiet after his run-in with Alice. She concentrated on chatting with her sister and, although Jane tried to bring others into their conversation, she couldn't manage it. Diane wasn't able to work up any enthusiasm for anything, and Josie acted as if she could barely wait until time to flounce out.

The minute the first person—Diane, I think it was—announced she had to leave, we all followed suit.

Don and I said little on the drive back to my house, and I wasn't surprised when he suggested he'd drop me off and go back to his own place. "I need some down time. That neighbor of Kate's didn't set well with me. Maybe a nap will help me get some Christmas spirit back. I'll give you a call later."

I didn't argue the point.

Suddenly I was home alone, at three o'clock on Christmas afternoon with the rest of the day uncommitted.

I knew what I wanted to do. I also knew my idea might have unforeseen repercussions. But when had I ever let possible repercussions stop me?

Half an hour later I walked into the Warren County jail at the Municipal Center, armed with a canister of Christmas cookies, and approached the clerk handling sign-ins at the reception desk. "I'm Mayor Graham from Emerald Point. I'd like to see Lucas Prendergast."

My request took her by surprise. "I don't know, Mayor. I'm not sure if anyone's supposed to see him today or not," she stammered.

She pushed open the door of a visiting room, already crowded with relatives and friends of the prisoners, and signaled to Sergeant Rick Cronin, the officer on duty.

Under different circumstances Rick, still in his twenties and the youngest man in the department, might have been easy to convince. But since he'd played a role in some of my recent misadventures, I primed myself for an argument.

He was shaking his head as he approached me. "I don't think Jim expected him to have visitors today, Mayor, so he didn't leave any orders on that. And I sure don't want to call him at home. He was wiped out when he left last night."

I waited. That wasn't quite a no, was it? "Rick, the man was a friend of my grandparents. I remember him from my visits to the lake years ago. I thought I'd bring him some cookies and find out if he needed anything."

Rick bit his lip. "I don't know what to say, Mayor."

"It's Christmas, Rick. Everybody else here seems to have company. If you don't feel comfortable putting him in the main visiting area, how about one of the small rooms? Could we do that? I'm sure he'll remember me."

"If I were to bring him out here, Mayor, he'd have to be in a place where the guards can keep a close watch on him. We're not sure about him yet." He stepped to the door of the visiting room and glanced around.

I stayed close behind him.

"We keep that last booth for prisoners who need to be isolated. I suppose you could meet with him there." He didn't sound convinced.

"That would be great, Rick. I appreciate this." Before he could change his mind, I followed him into the visiting room and plopped myself down in the chair on the visitors' side of the booth.

Rick hesitated again, then headed for the door which led into the jail.

For the next ten minutes I had nothing to do but glance around the room at the families who'd come to visit relatives on Christmas. What a sad day for everyone. One young woman, looking particularly bedraggled, juggled a baby on her lap as she struggled to hang on to a toddler who whined and tried to pull away from her. The man across from her had little to say, even to the children.

Next to her, an elderly couple squeezed onto one chair and made whispered comments to the young man across from them. Son or grandson? I couldn't begin to guess. A couple of girls, probably still in their teens, engaged in a silly exchange with a boy who didn't look old enough to be confined here rather than in a juvenile facility.

The room was hot, stifling hot; the air, stale and redolent of odors that didn't bear thinking about. I slipped off my jacket, wishing I'd left it in the waiting room.

I'd almost convinced myself I should leave and come back another time when the door at the far end of the room opened and two deputies appeared escorting a man dressed in the orange jump suit, which was apparently the required wear for inmates, even on Christmas. The prisoner trudged along, his head down, his movements impeded by the shackles on both his hands and feet. What I could see of his face appeared to be two different colors. His cheeks, weathered to a dull nut brown, were bordered by a white band running across his face just below his hairline and extending around his neck to the back of his head. As he came closer, I realized someone had cut his hair, probably while they were cleaning him up, and exposed skin which had been protected from the elements.

The guards guided him to the chair across from me and motioned to him to sit down. He responded to their directions awkwardly, but without objection. Once seated, he looked through the glass at me with no sign of recognition, then turned away to glance around the room with a puzzled expression. He showed no curiosity about who I was or why he'd been brought out of his cell for my visit.

When Henry Palmer, a guard whose family lived in Emerald Point, slipped the earphones onto his head, the prisoner's eyes darted quickly over my face. He said nothing, registered no emotion whatsoever.

Naturally, he wouldn't recognize me, I told myself. Why had I thought he might? I was a child the last time he saw me, and even if Rick had told him my name, he might not recall it.

What had I been thinking? The man I'd expected to see had existed in my memory for twenty-five years, exactly as he'd been on the last day I saw him. This man sitting across from me obviously didn't know me, and I couldn't know for sure he was the person I thought he was unless he at least remembered my name.

I leaned close to the mic and pressed the button. "Luke Prenders?" I said.

No answer. The blank stare didn't change.

"I'm Loren Graham. It's been a long time since we've seen each other." I rattled off my grandparents' names, told him where they'd lived on the lake, how he used to come by their house to sit on the porch with my grandfather, how much he'd liked my grandmother's chocolate cake and cookies. There was no response.

I plodded along, told him I'd brought some Christmas cookies the guard would give him after I left. "Don't expect them to taste anything like my grandmother's used to. Nothing like those chocolate chip ones she made that were so good. I wish I'd paid more attention when she tried to teach me to make them, but I didn't."

I thought I glimpsed a flicker of recognition at that, but he didn't respond.

I sat a few minutes longer.

He didn't speak, but he kept staring at my face.

I stood up, pushed my arms down into the sleeves of my jacket. "Good-bye, Luke." It hardly seemed a good time or place to wish him Merry Christmas, so I didn't. I signaled to the guard to indicate I was ready to leave and turned away.

"Lorie?" His voice was so low, I wasn't sure he'd spoken.

I turned back, waited.

"Lorie?" This time I knew what I'd heard. It was my childhood nickname, the name my grandmother often called me. Of course, it made sense that Luke, my grandparents' friend, would have called me that too. I'd almost forgotten.

"Yes. That's right. It's me—Lorie."

Henry Palmer and the other guard had come up behind him, ready to escort him back to his cell. Luke stared at me, but didn't say anything more. The guards helped him to his feet. Without another word, or even a backward glance, he shuffled off.

Chapter 6

A half hour later I was knocking on Kate's front door.

"Come in. It's open," she called out.

Kate huddled in her big recliner with her feet up and her eyes heavy with fatigue. The living room, restored to its usual perfect order, was lighted only by the glow from the old-fashioned bulbs on the Christmas tree and the evergreen wreaths in the two front windows. The room, warm and inviting, emanated the holiday spirit and tranquility I was hoping to find.

"You're not taking Jim's advice about keeping your door locked, I see. What if I was the murderer?"

"Kate lifted her head. " I saw you pull up so I was reasonably sure you weren't the murderer—unless you'd brought him along with you. I need someone to bring me back to life. Want a glass of wine."

"Love it. Tell me where it is, and I'll get it."

The jangle of the phone on the table next to her made us both jump.

"You know where I keep the wine and the glasses are on the counter." She motioned me toward the kitchen as she reached for the receiver.

I switched on a light in the kitchen and went straight to the low cupboard which Kate jokingly referred to as her wine cellar. I pulled out a corked bottle of Chardonnay, left from our Christmas brunch. The glasses we'd used had been washed and left upside down on a towel on the counter. I filled two of them with wine and carried them into the living room.

Kate, the receiver to her ear, made a series of grimaces at me as she listened to whatever her caller was telling her. Her mouth was set. When she finally spoke, her voice had a sharp edge. "I really can't talk now, Teddie. It's been a busy day. And you may be getting all upset over nothing. This is one of those things that can look a lot different in the morning."

I raised my eyebrows and gave her a questioning look, but Kate continued to listen, without acknowledging my curiosity. She murmured a few more phrases in that same cold tone she'd used before, then swung her arm out to hang up the phone.

I couldn't wait for her to volunteer information. "Teddie Murray's calling you on Christmas night? What's on her mind? Did you cater something for her she wasn't satisfied with?"

Before Kate could answer, the front door banged open. Diane Anderson, her dark hair hanging wet and untidy under a blue knit cap, burst into the room. "Loren, I went to your house first, then I thought maybe you were still here."

"Not still here. Making a return visit in case Kate hadn't seen enough of me today."

"I can't believe what's going on. Do you know Teddie Murray is calling people all over town about you? Caught me in the shower."

I glanced toward Kate. "She just called here too. I was asking Kate what she said. What do you mean she's calling people about me?" I said.

Kate's cheeks were flushed. Her fair complexion made it impossible for her to hide any feelings of embarrassment. Obviously, Teddie's phone call had hit on a hot-button topic.

Before Kate could answer, Diane jumped in. "Maybe this is all a misunderstanding. Tell me one thing, Loren. Did you go down to the jail today, demand to see the Woodsman and try to get him released on bail?"

"Did Teddie say that?"

Kate gestured toward the phone. "That's what she told me too. I was just about to tell you."

"I don't believe this. Yes, I went to see him—that part of the story is right—but no, I didn't demand anything, and I didn't try to get him released. And you think this is all over town already?"

"Thanks to Teddie. She's making it sound like you rushed down there to go to bat for him," Kate said.

Kate handed Diane her untouched glass of wine as I repeated the story I'd used at the jail. "He was a friend of my grandfather's, really kind to me when I used to come up here to visit as a kid. I took him some cookies. I didn't demand anything. I guess I did talk Rick Cronin into letting me see him, but that's it. And I definitely did not try to get him released."

"Okay, let me make sure I understand this," Diane, always the logical one, continued the questioning. "He was a friend of your grandfather's, kind to you when you were a kid, so that makes him innocent? Aren't you making a pretty big leap of faith here?"

Kate chimed in. "And Loren, even going to see him. Do you think that was wise?"

"The waiting room was full of visitors. It wasn't as if I was the only person there."

"But they weren't there to see him, were they? Weren't they people visiting their own families?" Diane pressed hard for an answer.

"I don't know that he has a family to visit him." I could feel prickles in my cheeks as my face grew hot.

Diane didn't let up "But Loren, you realize that the fact he was kind to you when you were a kid doesn't rule out the possibility that he's a murderer now. You do see that, don't you?"

Before I could snap at her, Kate brought the foot rest of the recliner down hard and pushed herself up. "Time for more wine. Let me have your glasses."

Diane and I handed Kate our glasses, and she headed for the kitchen.

"I don't know where Teddie is going with this," Diane said. "She's got a ton of relatives, and she obviously intends to make a big deal of you giving the Woodsman your support. You'd better be sure you've thought this whole thing through."

"When I step over these imaginary lines people draw around here, I usually only have Jim to contend with. You mean now I've added Teddie to my enemies list?" I tried for a light approach, but it didn't quite come off.

"Enemies list?" Kate said as she returned, balancing three glasses of wine

Diane nodded. "Teddie Murray, whether we believe her or not, has lots of friends and relatives who agree with everything she says. That gives her clout, and she doesn't always use it wisely."

"I'll second that. I've dealt with her." Kate clamped her mouth shut. She made it a point not to talk about the clients who used her catering service, but sometimes a comment slipped out. I got the message.

"Be careful, Loren. That's all I'm saying. Be very careful," Diane added.

"I will," I said.

But, of course, at that point, before everything had turned into a Class A mess, I didn't see any reason to put being careful on my agenda.

The next morning after a boring night alone, I decided I might as well go into work. Technically, the day after Christmas was considered a holiday by most of the village and county offices, so I was surprised when Pauline arrived a few minutes later.

"Somehow I thought you'd be here. You've heard about Teddie Murray's campaign, I take it," she said.

"I've heard. I'm not quite sure how to handle this. What do you think?"

Pauline settled herself in the chair next to my desk. In contrast to the dark slacks and top I'd grabbed out of my closet, she was decked out in one of her brightly colored Christmas sweaters, this one featuring reindeers galloping across the back and a chubby Santa Claus distributing brightly wrapped gifts to smiling children on the front. Her serious expression offered a sharp contrast to the cheerful scene.

"Loren, you know Teddie's related to more than half the town, and for reasons I don't understand, everybody in her family seems to listen to her. She could make a lot of trouble if you don't find a way to shut this gossip down."

"Both Kate and Diane have already read me the riot act. You realize most of what you've heard isn't true, don't you? I took the guy some Christmas cookies for old time's sake, because he was really kind to me years ago when I was visiting my grandparents."

"So you didn't try to get him released? I figured that might be a stretch."

"Pauline, no. I don't believe this town sometimes."

"How about the big hug and kiss? That not true either?"

"Of course not. In fact, I didn't think he even realized who I was at first, didn't have any idea until they were taking him back to his cell."

"You mean he seemed to know you then?"

"I couldn't be sure of that. I thought he said 'Lorie' once. Actually, I thought he said it a second time. That's what he used to call me, so I figured he might have been getting some sense of who I was."

"What else did he say? Does he know why he's in jail?"

"He didn't speak at all until they were taking him away. He looked back and said 'Lorie'. That was it."

"Well, you've done your duty by him. That gonna be the end of it, do you think, or you got something else in mind?" She gave me a look only Pauline could give.

I didn't know the answer to that question, so I didn't take a stab at it.

We puttered around for almost an hour, each of us in our own office, until I wondered what was the point in wasting the day.

"Let's go home, Pauline. There's really nothing here we need to do," I said.

"If you're sure."

"Tomorrow, I'll draw up an agenda for next week's council meeting and you can make copies of those new environmental regs I want to hand out to the members. We've got plenty of time on that."

She didn't give me a chance to change my mind. "See you in the morning then."

Pauline took off fast, and I followed right behind her.

Ten minutes later, I bypassed the road which led to my house and headed for the Upstate Medical Clinic located on the northern outskirts of town. I knew that Bobbie Smith, an Emerald Point girl and a nurse at Glens Falls Hospital, volunteered for a short stint there once or twice a week. Maybe, just maybe, she'd be working today.

The parking lot outside the long, white frame building was almost deserted, but I'd guessed right. Bobbie's bright green Toyota was tucked into the far row away from the entrance. Bobbie, the consummate professional, had not only come into work the day after Christmas, she'd left plenty of parking spaces near the entrance for patients seeking medical treatment for their post-holiday ailments.

Despite the stresses of the season, however, few people had turned up for medical help—unless they'd arrived en masse the first thing in the morning and had already been taken care of. I asked the young receptionist I didn't recognize if Bobbie could spare me a few minutes.

"I'm sure she can, Mayor Graham," she said, and ushered me into Bobbie's office immediately.

"Mayor Graham, I hope you're not ill." Bobbie turned away from the cabinet where she was arranging supplies and came forward to shake my hand.

To my surprise, she was not wearing her usual spanking white uniform and starched cap. Apparently even Bobbie had gone modern and switched to one of the attractive slacks outfits the medical supply companies now featured for nurses. Hers was simply cut and carefully tailored in a soft shade of rose, a perfect color choice for someone with her blue eyes and fair complexion, nothing like the gaudy smocks I'd noticed on some of the nurses at the hospital. Those, I knew, wouldn't be Bobbie's style.

I'd already worked out my explanation of why I was there. "No. I'm fine. I was heading up this way and got wondering how people here were reacting to the murder. The news must have been so upsetting, especially to some of the older people living on the mountain."

"Well, there has been a lot of talk," Bobbie said carefully

"And are people worried about another murder? Are they keeping their doors locked the way the Sheriff's Department suggested?"

"I hope so. Of course with the Woodsman in jail, some folks think the problem is solved, and there's no longer any need to worry." Bobbie studied my face as if she expected me to confirm or deny that statement.

I decided not to do either. "I hope people won't jump to conclusions. The Woodsman may have taken clothes and food from homes around here—I think we've all heard that—but that doesn't make him a murderer."

"Perhaps not, but half the town thinks of him that way. Lee Townsend—she worked with Denise McNaughton a lot—stopped in a little while ago. She was devastated by the news, but she came to see if we were overwhelmed with patients and needed help here in the clinic. She'd heard a lot of wild stories about the Woodsman already. People have been very quick to pin the murder on him, especially since they found some items from Denise's house in his lean-to. At least that's what Lee told me this morning."

I stood up and edged toward the door. "I'm sure there'll be all kinds of stories before this thing is over. I know I'll be keeping my door locked, and I hope everyone else will too."

Before Bobbie could say anything more, I was on my way out the door. She'd given me an idea, and the sooner I followed through on it, the better I was going to feel.

Lee Townsend lived on the northern fringe of Emerald Point in a big rambling farm house surrounded by a fenced yard, a house in desperate need of a fresh coat of paint on its clapboards and a dozen replacement shingles on its roof. I knocked on the front door.

"Come in," someone called."We're right here."

Lee was kneeling on the floor, stuffing two blonde-haired girls who looked to be three or four years old into bright purple snowsuits. "Santa Claus brought the twins these snowsuits yesterday, and they can't wait to get them on and go out to play. And they're not going to ask to come right back in either, are you, girls? I'm going to be talking to Mayor Graham for a while. Later we can go next door and show

Mary Alice your suits, but we won't go inside. That's how you catch cold, running in and out."

Lee opened the front door, and the girls waddled out. She watched them navigate the porch steps, then turned and picked up a chubby baby who'd been bouncing up and down in a Jolly Jumper. "The joys of winter. They'll be all right for about ten minutes and then they'll want to come in. So sit down, Mayor, while we have a minute, and tell me what I can do for you." She settled onto the couch with the baby on her lap and pointed to the cushion next to her.

I sat down "Lee, you've got a beautiful family, and I can see they're keeping you busy. I won't waste your time. You worked with Denise McNaughton, they tell me. Do you have any idea what happened in her life that might have led to her murder?"

"In other words, do I have any idea who killed her?"

She wasn't going to waste my time either. "Exactly. Did she have any enemies? Did she ever mention being afraid of anyone?"

Lee bounced the baby up and down without answering. We both smiled as he squealed with delight. Apparently, this was his favorite activity. She watched him for a minute or more, then began to speak slowly as if choosing each word with care. "I liked Denise a lot. We'd worked together for a long time. She was a terrific nurse—and a good friend to me when I needed one."

I would have liked to hear more on that subject, but first things first. I waited, hoping for a hint, a speculation, anything that might throw some light on Denise's murder. Nothing. I primed the pump.

"People speak so highly of Denise. Everyone says she was an outstanding nurse, really well thought of. It's hard to understand why someone would want to kill her."

She hesitated again before she answered. "I suspect you've heard she had a number of men friends. Am I right? That seems to have a lot of people really shook up."

"But not you?" I asked.

"Personally, I thought it was her own business, but people around here can be tough. Serial monogamy is okay, I guess, but juggle a couple guys at the same time, and you're trash."

"Is that what Denise was doing, do you think—seeing a couple of guys at the same time?" I leaned forward, and the baby grabbed for one of the buttons on my coat.

Lee reached for the child's hand and lifted it to her lips for a kiss. "He'd have that button off your coat and in his mouth before we knew it. What did you ask me?"

"If you thought she was involved with a couple of guys at the same time."

"She liked men. She liked the early days of a relationship, the falling in love stage where anything seems possible. Yes, I think she was in that stage with someone new."

"And she'd been seeing someone else?"

I waited again. When she didn't answer, I said, "Do you have any idea who the men were?"

"Not really. She definitely didn't want to name names. She made that pretty clear."

"You think because they were married?"

"Maybe in one case the guy was. But in another, I got the idea the man was single, or divorced maybe, judging by something she said. She still didn't want to say who it was."

"Did anyone ever ask her point blank."

"I didn't. I wouldn't do that, but I gave her a lot of chances to tell me."

"So she was really close-mouthed?"

"Denise didn't let down her hair about her personal life. Once in a while she'd mention going to some restaurant for dinner or on a weekend trip, but even if she did, she wasn't big on details. And I had the feeling she didn't want me to ask her a lot of questions."

"So you didn't ask," I said.

Her expression changed. "And now I wish I had. I'd like to see them catch whoever did this to her. I hate to think some bozo's going to get away with her murder."

"You're thinking it's a man who did it?" I asked.

"Women don't kill that way, do they?"

I thought about what she was saying. "I'm not sure what you mean?"

"Don't you read things about how women use different methods than men when they want to murder someone—poison maybe, or something less violent?"

"I guess," I said, but the saying, "Hell hath no fury like a woman scorned" came popping into my head. Could Denise have incurred some woman's wrath by appropriating her husband or boyfriend? Wasn't that a tried and true reason for murder, maybe for a violent one as well?

When I drove up to my house half an hour later, I was surprised to find the Christmas candles gleaming in all the windows and smoke from the fireplace billowing out the chimney. And as if that wasn't enough, when I opened the kitchen door, I was almost knocked off my feet by the delicious aroma wafting around the room. Don stood at the stove, grinning and stirring the contents of my bright red Dutch oven. Through the doorway to the living room, I could see a crackling fire in the fireplace and my coffee table set for two with my best place mats and china.

"I don't know what to do first—hug you or look in that pot you're stirring. This is truly a feast for the senses—you here and the promise of something superb for dinner."

I managed a big hug for him and, with only a few seconds delay, a peek inside the Dutch oven which turned out to contain a fabulous boeuf bourguignon—obviously from Kate's.

"I'm relieved to hear you say that after I was such a pain in the butt yesterday. I was afraid you'd feel as if I'd ruined our Christmas."

"I'd say Kate's friend managed that without much help," I said.

"I didn't have to let her get to me. Maybe if her husband had been there, she would have toned down the opinions. But let's not talk about that. I want to have a perfect Christmas dinner of our own—our first as an engaged couple, you realize." He filled one of my best wine glasses to the brim with Merlot and handed it to me.

I didn't comment that my refrigerator and freezer were still full of food from the party and that there was plenty of wine left as well. Instead, I helped him carry our filled plates and glasses, along with a basket of my favorite homemade bread, also from Kate's, into the living room.

What with the wine and the fire and the delicious food, it didn't seem a good time to bring up the Woodsman or the gossip making the rounds. And it didn't seem like a good time to mention where I'd been that day or to reveal that I'd started poking into Denise's murder. So I didn't.

After we'd finished eating, he reached behind him and produced a small gift box wrapped in gold foil. "I was sorry not to have this for Christmas. I ordered it early in November, but it got delayed somehow and didn't get here in time. The store called today to tell me it had finally come in."

I didn't know what to say to that, so I ripped off the paper and lifted the cover from the box. A pendant, an aquamarine which I guess I'd mentioned once was my birthstone, surrounded by small diamond chips on a delicate silver chain.

"It's exquisite," I said, and it was. I leaned forward and kissed him, and for once I didn't add anything stupid, didn't remind him how we'd agreed not to buy expensive gifts for each other this year or say anything else that would have spoiled the moment. Instead, I blinked back something that was scratching at my eyes and kissed him again with even more feeling.

"Stay right there," he said.

In minutes he'd transported the dishes to the sink, wrapped what was left of the bread in foil and, with only a few clinks and clatters and muttered swear words, squeezed the pot of boeuf bourguignon into the already overloaded refrigerator. He picked up the wine and our glasses and still managed to keep one arm tight around me as we walked upstairs.

As I sat down on the window seat in my bedroom, he poured us each another glass of wine and joined me in my nightly ritual of staring out at the lake. The vast expanse of sky, ablaze with the winter constellations so spectacular in this part of the world, arched above the dark water like one of those shows I used to love at the Planetarium. And when he kissed me, I felt the kind of Christmas warmth I'd wanted to feel the day before, felt a rush of gratitude for all that I had, for all the good things that had come to me since I'd moved to the lake and started a new life, first on my own and now with this gentle and loving man.

He took the glass out of my hand and with his arm around me again, led me over to the bed. When I slipped out of my clothes and under the covers, I realized he'd managed to turn on the electric blanket so that the bed was a warm, soft cocoon and as I pulled him down beside me and moved against him, I felt I had reached a safe haven at last after a long journey.

Chapter 7

I was still half asleep the next morning when I felt Don sit down on the bed next to me. As he handed me my favorite mug filled with coffee, I was surprised to see he was freshly shaved and dressed in a suit and tie.

"What time is it? Have I slept the day away? Why are you dressed like that?"

"Drink some coffee. I'll answer all those questions and in the proper order. It is a little before seven o'clock. No, you haven't slept the day away. I'm dressed like this because I'm off to Albany for a meeting. I didn't want to spoil our evening by talking about work, but there's been a problem with some of the proposed legislation and our committee needs to get together and find a solution."

"Will you have to stay over?" Don kept a small apartment in Albany for just this kind of emergency.

"Possibly. One night or even two. I'll call you when I know for sure."

"But... "

"Go back to sleep. You don't have to get up this early, do you? Don't drink the coffee, if you want to sleep in. I'll call you." He was out the door and gone before I could say anything more.

I didn't go back to sleep. Before the clock struck nine, I had showered and dressed and was guzzling my second cup of coffee at the kitchen table while I glanced through the morning paper. A quick knock at the door, and Josie Donohue, in true Josie fashion, came bursting into the room.

"Lor, you're supposed to keep your doors locked. Didn't you hear the warnings?"

"It was locked until ten minutes ago. I just went out to pick up the paper."

"I guess it's all right anyway as long as that Woodsman's still in jail."

"Don't say that, Josie. I hate the way everybody's got him tried and convicted without any evidence."

"Lor, they found the murdered woman's stuff in his hut. That's gotta mean something."

"They found a lot of other stuff there too, as I understand it, things that belong to people who are still alive."

"If you say so, Lor. I can't take time to argue. I'm here to ask a favor of you."

"So, ask," I said.

"Come to lunch with me. You said this wouldn't be a very busy week. Can you take a couple hours off?"

"We can have lunch right here. I've got a ton of leftover food from my party."

"No. I mean at my father's. He's invited me to have lunch with him at his house today, and I want you to come with me."

"Why?"

"I told him I wanted you to meet him. He said he'd like to meet you too some time, and I should ask you to come with me today."

"Why do I think there's a catch here some place?"

"No catch, Lor."

"So why today?"

"Well, you're good at finding out things from people. Maybe you can find out where he was when I went up to his house the night before the concert."

"You mean the night of the murder?"

"If you have to put it that way. I really would like to know where he was."

I could hardly refuse that invitation, could I? I agreed to go.

Josie, who insisted on driving, picked me up at my office, and we headed north. Tim rented a double wide trailer on one of those poorly maintained side roads that could have been part of Mountainside or not, depending on the whim of the early settlers when they drew up the town lines.

He greeted us warmly with a big hug for Josie and a handshake for me. "Good to meet you, Loren. Josie has told me some great things about you. I'm glad you could come."

Josie began a quick recall of the Christmas dinner she'd shared with Tim's family. "That side of the family all talk at once, and they never stop. Dad and I hardly got a chance to say anything to each other at all that night. That's why he suggested I have lunch with him today. He wants to hear more about the Holiday Concert, don't you Dad?"

"Didn't she do a beautiful job with her solo?" I said, relieved to jump quickly into a comfortable topic.

"Terrific. She wowed me anyway. I was impressed." Tim gave her shoulders a squeeze.

While Josie chattered on about the concert and some of the comments made about it afterward, Tim pulled out chairs for us at the table and stepped into the kitchen area to begin dishing up the lunch. As he busied himself at the counter, I had my first chance to look at him close up. If he'd abused alcohol and drugs, as people believed, he'd escaped their ravages. At forty-five, he could easily have passed for ten years younger. He was close to six feet tall, well-built and muscular, with dark hair, no sign of gray, and a smooth, clear complexion. It was easy to see why he might have slipped into the role of ladies' man.

"Want to take this for me, Josie?" He slid a plate of crispy fried chicken across the counter. "And this." He produced a bowl of tossed salad and a crock of baked beans.

"Dad makes great baked beans. Wait 'til you try them," Josie said.

"I was a cook years ago at the Sagamore Resort," Tim said as he sat down with us. "Learned a lot from the chef. That's how Kate and I met—both of us worked there one summer."

"I didn't know that. That's where Kate started cooking?"

"She was a waitress first, but she took every chance she got to help in the kitchen. Wasn't long before they asked her to do some food prep." As we ate, Tim rambled on about his years working at the lake. Josie hung on his every word, as if anxious to learn all she could about his life.

When we'd finished the ice cream cake Tim produced for dessert, she suddenly thought of something she wanted to show him, something she'd left in the car. As she got up from the table to go after it, she paused long enough to give me a meaningful look and a painful kick in the ankle.

This was my cue to question Tim, but since I had no idea how to introduce the subject Josie wanted discussed, I found myself at a loss. Before I could think of a way to steer the conversation to where he'd been the night of the murder, he turned the tables. "So you've got something you want to talk to me about. Right?"

"What do you mean?" I stammered.

"I'm just getting to know Josie, but she's pretty transparent some times. I'd say you're either about to tell me something, probably about

Kate, or ask me questions I'd be more apt to answer if Josie wasn't here."

He'd almost hit the mark. I grabbed for a safe topic. "Josie takes pride in her detecting skills. She must get them from you. Maybe she was a little heavy-handed today, but I think she's trying to figure out if you're going to stick around for a while. And I suspect she's hoping you and Kate might get back together."

"I know she'd like assurances, but I can't give them. I've got a job cooking at Danville's Restaurant in Lake George Village, but business isn't very good, and there's no guarantee they'll keep me on from one week to the next. Winter's always a slow time at the lake—Josie must know that from Kate's experiences. As far as Kate and I are concerned, even if I wanted to imagine that possibility, I'm afraid I don't see it happening, do you?"

No way was I falling into that trap. "That's a loaded question, if I ever heard one. I wouldn't dream of trying to answer it."

"Of course you can't. Sorry. But I would like to talk to you sometime. Not now, with Josie apt to bounce in the door any minute. Would you be willing to let me come by and tell you about a decision I have to make, see how you think I should handle it?"

My instinct was to refuse, but my feelings for Kate and Josie held me back. "I haven't made the best decisions about my own life, but sure, I'll take a stab at anything."

"I don't want to come to your office when Pauline's there, or anybody else for that matter. What if I came to your house?"

"Well, no one's apt to be in the office early, especially this week. What if you stopped in about nine o'clock?"

"Great," he said, as Josie slid the door open and poked her head in.

"I'm back. I've brought the write-up about our concert from the paper, Dad, in case you didn't see it." She handed him a clipping encased in a plastic page holder.

Tim studied the clipping as if it revealed the secrets of nuclear fission and paused after every line or two to second the reviewer's praise. I added my two cents with emphasis on how well Josie had done and what a hit her performance was.

By the time we left that afternoon, Jessie was glowing with pride, giving me a glimpse once again of the lovely, confident woman she could become. Our good-byes were warm and friendly. On the drive home, I expected her to be disappointed at my failure to find out where Tim had been the night of the murder, but to my surprise, she wasn't as distressed as I thought she'd be.

"I think you're right, Lor. He probably went to an AA meeting or something like that. I'd still like to know for sure, but it's no big. Let's not worry about it anymore."

Since my worry about plunging to my death on the winding mountain road was enough to occupy me right then, I agreed.

At a little before nine o'clock that night, I'd snuggled down in my big recliner to read the latest Dana Stabenow novel and half-watch a recap of the day's news. The house was freezing cold, not surprising since the outside temperature hovered around zero and the wind was howling off the lake with a ferocity that set my windows rattling like castanets. Rather than ask more of the furnace which showed its age and infirmities on nights like this, I'd put on my pink terrycloth robe over my clothes and pulled my grandmother's old Granny Square afghan onto my lap.

Nine o'clock is late on a winter's night at the lake, so I was surprised when the doorbell rang, even more surprised to find Tim Donohue standing outside my back door blowing on his hands and stamping his feet.

"Tim, what's wrong?"

"I need to talk to you, Loren. It's important."

I hesitated for a second or two, but any reluctance I felt about inviting him in was counter-balanced by the possibility I'd freeze to death if I didn't get the door closed fast. I stepped back and motioned him into the kitchen.

"I appreciate you seeing me, Loren. I won't stay long, I promise. I need advice and I can't think of anyone else I'd trust enough to talk to."

"I thought you were going to come to the office in the morning." The good will I'd felt for him that afternoon evaporated. Something about his visit this late in the evening hit me wrong.

My comment surprised him. Either that or else he delivered a masterful piece of acting. "I thought you meant for me to come here tonight. I told you I didn't want to run into Pauline or anybody else."

I struggled to recall our conversation. It had been a little fuzzy—I conceded that fact—so I pulled out a chair for him at the kitchen table and sat down across from him. "All right. Sit down then. Tell me what's on your mind."

"The murder. That's what on my mind. I'm scared to death they're going to try to pin it on me. A lot of people around here don't think much of me, you know, and I lived right near Denise on the mountain.

They probably have me listed as the prime suspect already."

"But why would you be a suspect, Tim? You're not saying they'd suspect you because you lived near her, are you? That would be a stretch."

He looked down at his hands as he unzipped his coat. His movements were slow and awkward as if he were trying to delay his answer as long as he could. He was still struggling with the bottom of the zipper when he muttered, "I was seeing her."

"Seeing her? What the hell does that mean?" I was too tired for euphemisms.

"Seeing her, spending time at her place."

I gave a disgusted snort and started to get up.

He got the message. "Okay, you want me to admit I was sleeping with her. Yes, I was. But she insisted we keep it quiet, and that was all right with me. I didn't want Josie and Kate to find out."

"So how long had this been going on? You met her after you moved back here?"

"She ran sometimes in the morning. We'd see each other on the road. One morning she asked me if I wanted to come back to her house for coffee. That started it. She was fun to be with. I liked her attitude. She'd heard the talk about me and Kate, told me not to let it get me down."

"The talk?"

"You must have heard it too, Loren. That I was no good, that I came back to ruin Kate's life, her business too maybe. One story was I wanted to be her partner, get my guilty paws on everything she'd built up."

"Really? I admit this is a bad place for talk, but I never heard that."

"You can bet Kate heard it. I'd wager a lot of well-meaning people warned her off me."

I thought about Josie. I wondered how much of this she'd heard and what her reaction had been. "So how long were you with Denise?"

"A couple of months, not every day, not that steady. Sometimes at night she'd let me stay over, but I think she was seeing someone else too."

"Do you know who it was?"

"No. I asked her once, but she told me it was none of my business."

The light began to dawn. "Josie told me she drove up to your place the night before the concert to make sure you knew about it, and you weren't there. Were you at Denise's house that night? That was the night of the murder. You mean you were with her then?"

"I know this looks bad, Loren. I did go up there, but she wasn't home. I'd called her that day and she told me she was busy that night, but I went anyway."

"Why? Why would you do that?" As if I'd never felt that kind of desperation myself.

"I really wanted to see her. I waited around for a while and then left."

"How long did you wait? Josie went to your house after ten o'clock. You mean you waited until later than that?"

"Denise worked three to eleven most of the time. She didn't get home until midnight or after."

"You're telling me you waited there from before ten until after midnight? Where did you wait? Were you able to get in the house?"

"I sat in my car. I swear it. I never went in the house. It didn't seem strange she didn't come home. I knew she worked over sometimes. I figured that's what she was doing."

"And that's the night she was killed?"

"That's the night. And now I'm afraid somebody saw me there, somebody else she was seeing. Maybe he saw me waiting for her and that set him off. Maybe that's why she was killed."

"Did you see anyone else, any other cars around?"

"No, but that doesn't mean anything. There a million places up on that mountain somebody could pull off the road. There could even have been someone waiting in the house."

"How? You mean there were lights on in the house?"

"Only a couple of low lights she always left on when she went to work."

"Damn it, Tim. That story wouldn't hold up at all with the sheriff's department. You weren't home at ten o'clock when Josie went to your house. Yet you say Denise wouldn't have finished her shift and driven back to her house until after midnight. You expect me to believe you sat in your car for over two hours waiting for her in weather like this when you knew she wouldn't come home anyway?"

"No, no. You're right. I went to a bar. I didn't drink, I swear I didn't, but sometimes it's just better to be around people."

"So somebody must have seen you there."

"Even if they had, I left at eleven. Loren will you help me? I can't go around asking questions—that would really start people suspecting me—but you can."

"You want me to ask questions? What questions?" I'd met this guy for the first time only a few hours before. He sure didn't lack for nerve.

"You could find out who Denise was seeing, find out if she was with him that night. If she was, he's probably the one who killed her."

"That's quite a jump, Tim."

"Okay, maybe it is. But that guy probably knows something. "Please, Loren, will you help me? I don't care why you do it, do it for Josie or Kate even, if you don't want to do it for me."

I didn't know how to answer him. I'd started out wanting to prove Luke Prendergast innocent of Denise's murder. Now Tim thought he was a suspect, and he wanted me to help him. But if Tim was innocent and I helped him prove it, wouldn't Luke go back to being the number one suspect?

My thoughts were in a jumble. I needed time to sort them out. "Tim, you've got to give me a day or two to decide about this."

He began to say something else, but I stopped him. "No. You've got to back off, give me time to think this through. I can't decide tonight. You have to leave now, right now." I stood up.

To his credit, he didn't protest. "Okay, Loren. At least you heard me out—I wasn't even sure you'd be willing to do that much. I thank you for that. But I'm telling you—find out who she was sleeping with and you'll find her killer."

He tugged open the back door. A blast of cold air slammed into me, but I followed him into the entranceway. I leaned against the frame of the outer door and watched him as he started down the walk.

After a few steps, he turned back as if to say something more. When he did, a car parked across the street started up with a roar and pulled away from the curb.

There was no reason for a car to be parked there, especially at this time of night. I couldn't see who was in it, couldn't make out a license number as it sped off. I couldn't hear what Tim said then either, but I didn't care. I'd already heard enough to keep me awake half the night.

Chapter 8

After Tim left, I made myself a cup of cocoa, skimmed through several chapters of a very bad romance novel and kept my mind as empty of disturbing thoughts as I could. I even managed to fall asleep without dredging up the high points of our conversation.

Despite my efforts, I was awake early, too wired to lie in bed one minute longer. I stumbled down to the kitchen, made a pot of coffee and thought through what Tim had told me, and how it applied to Denise and her life in Mountainside.

Local gossip had often linked her to men. No surprise there. However, she was discreet about her affairs, secretive actually, never inclined to reveal much information about her personal life. Most people who knew her conceded those facts. But this was a small town, and the people who lived here had many ties to one another, some of them unknown to the rest of us. There had to be people who knew the name of the man Denise was seeing—to borrow Tim's word. The question was—who knew and how would I ferret out the information.

Sheriff's Investigator Jim Thompson probably deserved top billing on the list, but discovering what he knew wouldn't be easy. In fact, when Jim wasn't ready to disclose something, getting anything out of him was virtually impossible. He'd have to be scratched off the list, at least temporarily.

Denise's two co-workers I'd talked to—Bobbie Smith and Lee Townsend—had not been at all forthcoming. If they knew the name of Denise's mysterious lover, they weren't willing to reveal it. They'd join Jim at the bottom of my list, at least for now.

With my next thought, however, I hit pay dirt. Ramona Dolley, lifelong friend of my grandmother's, now a good friend of mine, had lived in Emerald Point her entire life and knew everyone and everything. And Ramona would be expecting me to make a Christmas call sometime this week. Why not today?

I waited until a decent hour, then called to ask if I could stop by her house for a visit, When she agreed, I jumped in and out of the shower and took off. I didn't have to bother with breakfast. Ramona would have a cart load of delicious Christmas goodies ready to serve any guest who showed up.

Before I had a chance to knock, she pulled open her front door and wrapped me in a bear hug. Ramona, short, plump and gray-haired, always reminded me of the grandmother doll in the dollhouse family I'd loved as a child. Her husband Deke, who'd resembled both Ramona and the grandfather doll, had died under tragic circumstances several years before. To Ramona's credit, she'd pulled herself together, leased her cabin business to an area entrepreneur and managed to hang onto her house.

Once we'd settled ourselves at the table in Ramona's old-fashioned kitchen, we asked each other the mandatory questions about health, Christmas activities and plans for the next few months with emphasis on my forthcoming marriage to Don. During this exchange, I ingested a mind-boggling assortment of seasonal goodies, washed down with several cups of Ramona's delicious coffee.

Then, while I was still able to speak, I turned the conversation to the murder and possible suspects. Ramona didn't hesitate to lay her opinions on the table.

"Nice woman, that Denise," she said as she refilled my coffee cup once again. "Everyone spoke well of her, except for her carryings-on with men. Some folks up here still don't cotton to that kind of life. Do you think that's why someone wanted to kill her?"

"I was counting on you to know the answer to that question, Ramona. Any ideas?"

"There's been talk. Of course, there's always talk when something like this happens. 'Spect you've heard plenty of it already."

"So you asking me or are you about to tell me?" I said.

"Both. First, do you have any ideas? I suspect you've been nosin' around like you always do when murder hits up here."

"I've asked a few questions. No sense lying to you about that, Ramona. You know me too well. But I've found out zilch."

"What's wrong with Pauline? Doesn't she have any ideas? Don't tell me she and Reggie aren't in the know on this."

"I haven't found out anything from that quarter so far. That's why I'm here asking the expert."

Ramona gave me the raised-eyebrow look that meant she saw

through me, but she didn't let my blatant flattery stop her. "Some folks think she was involved with a couple of guys at the same time, and one of them was jealous enough to kill her rather than share her."

"Really?" I said. Responses like really were to Ramona like gasoline to a fire.

"I wouldn't be surprised if that theory will turn out to be the right one, but so far nobody's named anybody," she said

"So, who could name somebody, would you say?"

"I can tell you who could do it if he was of a mind to—Billie Jorgensen. He gets a lot of news down at that radio station. I'd bet my last dollar on it."

"So how long will it be before Billie spills what he knows? The man loves to talk."

"Don't count on it 'til he's ready. He won't want to tip off the other stations before he can go on the air with the story himself. Remember that big announcement about the Woodsman. He sat on that one all night, I heard, so he could announce it on his early morning newscast. Ratings went right through the roof that day, according to Joe Stevenson."

"So you're saying Billie might know, but I'd have to figure a way to get it out of him. Any ideas on how and where to do it?"

"Come on Loren, you're not losing your detectin' skills, are you? Where would be the easy part. You'd start at that greasy spoon down near the radio station. I've heard he stops in most days for a couple of beers around four-thirty or so, and then eats his dinner there before he goes back to do the evening news broadcast."

"Really?" Ramona was on a roll. That one word was still all I needed to keep it going.

"I've heard one of the countermen helps Billie with his phrasing. Tony Maloney—he's a colorful guy, used to be an English professor at a college, they say, fallen on hard times. Billie tells him the high points of a story and Tony helps him with the wording. That's how he creates that sense of hot-off-the-press coverage."

I was impressed, and I didn't try to hide it. "Ramona, how do you know all this stuff?"

"Keeping my ears open, Missy, just like you do. Maybe I even hear stuff people don't want to tell the mayor."

And in this town it might not be because people wouldn't tell the mayor. It might be because they wouldn't tell a newcomer like me who'd only been around for ten years, to say nothing about all those summers I spent here with my grandparents as a kid. Hardly a blip on the evolutionary time line in Emerald Point.

But that didn't mean I couldn't knuckle down and find out myself.

Before I left Ramona's, I telephoned the station. The switchboard operator gave me the word. Billie wouldn't be available until after he'd taken his supper break and finished the evening news broadcast. Ramona's time line appeared to be right on.

With Don away I could turn up at Sam's Diner about the same time Billie did and treat myself to somebody else's cooking in the bargain. Double dipping.

I'd always suspected Sam's might be on the opposite end of the fine dining spectrum from Kate's, and my suspicions were right. The minute I walked in the door, I realized this was not an eatery for the faint of heart or weak of gall bladder. Two guys were already chowing down at the long, wooden bar. A few other patrons, all men, were seated at three or four of the tables surrounding it. Among the popular choices, I spotted fried foods oozing large quantities of fat and eggs struggling to stay afloat in a sea of bacon grease.

I sat down at a table and pulled out one of the menus stacked against the chrome paper napkin holder. Since I knew from area gossip that Sam's fried meats had been the scourge of many a digestive track, I was relieved to see turkey featured as one of the specials and the cream pies I'd heard Sam's mother turned out for him every morning listed for dessert. If I fortified myself with a glass of beer and kept my wits about me, I could do dinner and maybe even take a piece of pie home.

Tony Maloney, who was tending bar, ambled over to take my order. "Whatever's on tap," I told him.

He returned in a few minutes and delivered my beer and a dish of peanuts.

"How long you been working here, Tony?" I'd figured the question as a casual conversation-starter, but Tony took it to heart.

"It's all I can get, Ms. Graham. I came back here thinking I'd pick up a teaching job. I taught downstate for a while, have the qualifications for high school English, but nobody wants to hire me."

"I'm sorry to hear that. I've got a friend teaches at Lake George. I understand a couple of people will be leaving at the end of the year. I'll ask her if she's got any ideas for you."

"That would be great. I'd appreciate it," he said and went back to the bar.

I'd no more than taken my first swallow of beer when Billie Jorgensen shoved open the front door and sauntered over to the table next to mine

Although I'd seen Billie many times before, I was always struck by the range of ancestors who'd contributed to his gene pool. He was short, squat, rough-featured, devoid of any beauty of face or form. The guy had almost nothing going for him—until he spoke. Then everything changed. His voice was rich in timbre, melodious even, each word, each syllable pronounced distinctly. People took lessons to get a voice like that. As far as anyone around here knew, Billie had managed to acquire his on his own. Radio was a perfect spot for him. He'd never cut it on TV, but radio was his niche.

Here at Sam's, Billie ranked as both an expected and revered dinner patron. Sam himself drew a beer and hustled it over to his table with his recommendation. "Got a great venison stew tonight, my man."

"That from the same buck you were bragging on yesterday?" Billie asked him.

"The same, and it's been a good one. Given five stars easy by everyone who's tried it."

I couldn't pass up a chance to comment. "You keep track of which deer your venison comes from?"

Both men looked at me as if I'd bottomed out on the stupid scale. "That's right. You're a city girl, aren't you Mayor? Your grandfather would turn over in his grave if he heard that question," Sam said.

Maybe so, but I'd elbowed my way into the conversation. I made a few remarks about venison, and in a minute I changed the subject. "By the way, Billie. I caught your announcement early the other morning after your all night broadcast. Woke me up with a jolt before daylight."

Billie preened. "The report came in around midnight, but if I'd broadcast the name at that time, every other station would have picked up on it by morning. Would have been old news by then and nobody would have cared who had it first."

I had no idea if this was proper broadcast ethics, but I could understand his reasoning. "But you cared. Right?"

"Damn straight. And when our ad staff cranks up their campaign this month, they'll care too. They'll make me look like another Tom Brokaw. That's the kind of thing brings in advertising, you know."

Now that Billie was on a roll, I posed the question I'd been wanting to ask. "Have you learned anything more about the Woodsman? I figured out right away who he is—friend of my grandfather's years ago. Must be other folks around here who remember him too."

Billie set down his beer. I had his full attention now. "You saying he was friends with old Mr. Graham?"

"Sure am. I remember him from when I was a kid. He'd sit on the porch and shoot the breeze with my grandfather for hours at a time. Helped me out of a tight spot one time even."

"That why you went down to the jail on Christmas and asked to see him?"

"You don't miss much, do you Billie?" I said.

"Don't miss anything, if I can help it."

I considered buying him a beer, but decided that would be too obvious. Instead I said "I don't know about you, but I don't see him as a murderer."

Before Billie could respond, Sam swung through the door from the kitchen carrying Billie's plate of venison stew, along with a basket of rolls and a bottle of hot sauce. "Here you go, Billie. And there's plenty more where this came from. Want another beer with it?"

Billie eyed the plate in front of him. "If I'm going to do justice to this, I guess I'll need another. Put everything on my tab as usual."

"You want another beer, Mayor? And a plate of venison too?" Sam said.

"This beer's all I got time for tonight, Sam I'll see how many stars Billie gives the stew. Maybe I'll come back another day."

Sam brought out the beer and disappeared into the kitchen. Billie busied himself with mashing up chunks of potatoes and vegetables and cutting the meat. I waited until he'd buttered a roll and doused his entire plate with hot sauce.

As soon as he'd wolfed down the first few bites, I decided it was safe to speak. "You know, Billie, I just can't see the Woodsman as a murderer. I remember him when I was a kid. He was always such a quiet, gentle guy. They've got to have some other suspects, wouldn't you say?"

Billie kept shoveling in his stew. "I expect they'll be checking out some of those folks at the hospital."

I couldn't resist digging deeper. "Anybody in particular, do you think?"

"Sure. Victim was a nurse. Worked the recovery room as I understand it. Got your surgeons coming in to check on their patients, wear those green surgical gowns, caps pushed up on their heads. Drives some of those nurses wild, I hear tell."

"Really?" I said.

Billie buttered another roll.

"Especially when it's one of those good-looking docs, I suppose." I was fishing shamelessly, not at all sure what I might catch, or even if it would be something I could keep or would want to throw back.

Billie smirked. "You mean like the kind gives his wife a terrific gift on Christmas Eve and then takes the girlfriend skiing at Gore on Christmas Day? You got to be smooth to pull that stuff off, you know."

"Smooth, or not very smart. Gore's not that far away. Lots of chance of being seen," I said.

"Some don't care whether they're seen or not. Maybe like rubbing the wife's nose in it." Billie mopped up the last puddle of gravy, drained his beer glass and stood up.

"I hate to think you're right," I said.

"How about I call you in a day or two for more background on the Woodsman, Mayor? That might make us a good feature no matter how this thing pans out."

"Sure," I said as he lumbered off.

At that point I not only wasn't hungry for venison stew, I wasn't at all sure I could ever eat anything again. I slipped on my coat and went over to the counter to pay for my beer.

"I'd sure appreciate it if you asked that friend of yours about jobs at the school," Tony said as he rang up my modest tab. "You get me a good lead, next time you come in, the venison dinner will be on me."

"I'll be glad to ask, Tony. No dinner necessary." I tried to put all thoughts of venison stew out of my mind and bolted out the door at top speed

Chapter 9

I was convinced when I left Sam's Diner I would never eat again, but impossible as it seemed, by the time I reached my house, I'd started feeling pangs of hunger. I poured myself a glass of wine, tossed together the lightest Caesar salad I could concoct and sat down at my kitchen table to go over what I'd learned from my conversation with Billie Jorgensen.

The phrase—skiing at Gore Mountain—kept bouncing around in my brain. A doctor had not only taken a woman with whom he was linked romantically skiing on Christmas, but he'd chosen to take her to a very nearby, very public ski resort which was probably filled with people who'd recognize him.

By the kind of coincidence which often happens in Emerald Point—and maybe for all I know in many other places in the world as well—I knew someone who might have seen them there. I put in a call to my young friend Josie Donohue. I didn't waste words. "Did I understand you to say you and Tommy took a ride up to Gore on Christmas Day? See anybody interesting?"

"Sure. The place was packed."

"Anybody stand out in the crowd?"

"Did my mother tell you? I saw Dr. Kennison skiing up there, big as life, having a great time for himself. Remember how his wife claimed the reason he couldn't come to the brunch was because he was serving that Men's Dinner at their church, doing a good deed on Christmas like the great guy he is?"

"You saying he wasn't?"

"Scratch that. He was hittin' the slopes big time at Gore."

I couldn't resist asking. "Alone?"

"How could I tell, Lor? Like I said, the place was mobbed."

So that didn't prove anything. "Maybe he'd finished serving the dinner by then. What time did you see him?"

"Not long after I left my house. I picked Tommy up and we drove up there to see if some of his friends were there."

"Were they?"

"Yeah. We found 'em, hung out in the lodge with them for a couple of hours. Saw Doctor K. when we first got there and again when we were leaving. Why you asking, Lor? You onto something?"

"No, no. Wondering, that's all."

"Sounds to me like you may have a big idea spinning around your brain. Want me to come over and wonder with you?" she asked.

"Not tonight. But thanks anyway," I said and hung up fast.

What I was occupying myself with that night was nebulous, free-floating speculation, some of which of necessity involved Josie's father. Why should I waste time wondering what Dr. Kennison was up to on Christmas Day when I could be worrying about Tim Donohue and his liaison with Denise McNaughton. The sheriff's department must know about their relationship by now. It was just a matter of time before Tim got hauled in for questioning and the news became public Then Kate and Josie would be caught up in the thick of things. I'd wondered if Kate was being too hard on Tim, but maybe she had him figured perfectly.

The next morning I drove down to Queensbury for a holiday visit to my friend, Investigator Jim Thompson of the Warren County Sheriff's Department. Since no one was guarding his outer office—looked like a slow week everywhere around the county—I tapped on the inner door and pushed it open.

"Okay if I come in, Jim?" I called. "I wanted to drop off some Christmas cookies. I remembered how much you liked these."

Jim rarely showed emotion, but since I'd arranged his acknowledged favorites, the double chocolate chip peanut butter bars, at the top of the basket—and made sure they were clearly visible through the cellophane wrappings—he couldn't suppress a smile.

"You want something, Mayor, and you don't mind being obvious about it. Why don't we save time and you just tell me what it is."

"I'm sure you can guess, Jim. I'd like to see the Woodsman again. Rick probably told you I visited him on Christmas. Not sure if he knew who I was that day or not."

"You two are old buddies, I understand." Jim eyed the cookies as he spoke.

"Friend of my grandfather's. Spent a lot of time rocking on the porch with him on summer afternoons."

"While you were doing what?'

"Playing, hanging out. I was only a child. Let me loosen those wrappings for you."

When he didn't say no, I reached across the desk, parted the sheets of cellophane and folded them back. The cookies glistened. Kate's finest, guaranteed irresistible.

Jim picked up two of his favorites. "Join me, Mayor. Unless of course you've poisoned these."

"Let me prove I haven't." I reached for one, avoiding any of Jim's top rated.

Once Jim was occupied with the cookies, I saw no point in wasting time. "How are you doing with Denise McNaughton's murder investigation?" I asked him.

"We're making progress." The standard answer.

"You've got some leads, I hope."

"As one of the deputies described them the other day, 'too many, and not good enough.' That comment sums up the case about as well as possible."

"I guess I don't understand what that means," I said, hoping for more.

"I'm sure you can figure it out, Mayor. Go visit your old friend. But keep this in mind when you do—all the cookies in the world won't help you if you find out something I should know and don't tell me."

No smile with that ultimatum. Not even a thank you for the cookies.

I took off fast.

The jail was located in the same complex as the sheriff's office, but once I'd left the building and the wind hit me again, I decided to drive over there rather than walk. The temperature had plummeted to a brutal low. Icy blasts whistled across the parking lot and grounds, scooping up the top layer of snow and whirling it around in the open spaces to create miniature white-outs. My face stung and my hands inside my gloves ached with cold before I could tug the heavy glass door open and slip inside. A few yards from the entrance, a deputy I didn't recognize was manning a desk.

"I'm Mayor Graham from Emerald Point, and I'm here to see Lucas Prendergast." I chose a polite, but firm approach. Sometimes it's a good idea to throw some weight around. Just not too much.

"Who the heck is that?" he asked.

"The news media is calling him the Woodsman, but that's his given name."

The deputy wrinkled up his nose as he checked through some papers, then made a phone call. "It's okay. You're cleared to see him, Mayor," he said when he hung up.

The procedure was the same as it had been on Christmas Day although Rick Cronin was not in evidence. I was escorted to a seat in the visiting room and asked to wait.

When Luke arrived, he was in shackles again, but he appeared cleaner and neater than he had the first time I saw him. I suspected he'd had another shower, a better shave, maybe even a haircut, but he seemed more agitated than he had on Christmas. His eyes darted around the room, first at me and then toward the guards stationed near the doors. Today I was the only visitor.

"I brought you some more cookies, Luke. I think they'll bring them to you after I leave

When he didn't reply, I rambled on. "I hope you got the ones I left for you Christmas Day. The guards took them to check on them. I guess they're afraid of what I might bring you."

He continued to stare at me without any sign of comprehension.

"I thought you remembered me when I came to see you on Christmas. I thought you called me Lorie."

Still no response."You used to come visit my grandfather at the lake. John Graham. You and he were friends, good friends. You two would sit out on the deck and talk about all kinds of things."

"John Graham."

It didn't sound like a question. Encouraged, I pressed on. "Yes. That was my grandfather. I've come to see if you need anything, if I can help you in some way. Do you have an attorney to represent you?"

No answer.

"Do you need anything? Can I bring you something?"

"John Graham."

"That's right. My grandfather."

Nothing more. He began looking around the visiting room again. I wondered if he were trying to figure out where he was and how he'd ended up in this strange place.

"Cookies?" he said after a few minutes. "You brought me cookies?"

"They'll give them to you when you get back in your cell."

"All right." He stood up.

Maybe the cookies hadn't been such a good idea after all. I signaled to the guard that I was going to leave. "Take care, Luke. I'll come back another time."

As soon as the guard joined us, I hurried out of the visiting room. When I reached the entrance, I pulled my scarf up around my ears and tucked my chin as far down into my coat collar as I could get it. I shoved open the outside door. My eyes watered from the cold as I dashed into the parking lot and headed for my car. Suddenly, a horn blared only a few feet away from me. I reared back, startled by my near collision with a sheriff's car.

Two deputies glared at me from the front seat, but I scarcely noticed them. Instead I stared at the prisoner being transported in the back. At first all I could see was a black ski jacket and a face, pale as death, peering back at me. Then the man began to make frantic movements as if he wanted to give me a message. I could see his lips move, but I couldn't decipher what he was saying. He shifted in the seat and moved closer to the window. He lifted his hands to me like a supplicant. I saw the handcuffs then and, as he pressed closer to the glass, I realized who he was. The prisoner was Tim Donohue.

Chapter 10

It was almost the three o'clock closing time, but Kate's coffee shop was still open for business when I dashed in twenty minutes later. As soon as Herb the Baker, the roly-poly counterman, handed me a mug of coffee, I pushed open the door to Kate's kitchen.

Kate was drizzling dark chocolate frosting over a tray of sumptuous looking éclairs, one of the desserts her customers always requested. She looked up with a smile. "Hi, Loren. Nice surprise."

As I cast around for the best way to break the bad news, the back door slammed open and Josie, out of breath and visibly distraught, barged through it. "Dad's been arrested," she cried.

"Josie, calm down. What makes you think so?" Kate, accustomed to emergencies of all kinds in her catering business, had mastered the art of keeping her cool in the most trying circumstances.

"Two deputies went to his house. They were going in just as I got there. Remember I told you he invited me there for lunch. So I pulled around to the back of the house and waited."

"Slow down. Take a breath. And…"

"They were in there for a few minutes, not very long at all. When they came out, there was one on each side of him. He was handcuffed and they were hanging onto his arms. They shoved him into the back seat of their car. They even did that thing they do on TV when they push somebody's head down as they put him in a car."

Kate pulled one of the stools out from under the counter and sat down hard. "I thought he was trying to stay off everything."

"I came to tell you this too, Kate. I was there when they brought him to the jail," I said.

"How, Loren? Why were you there?"

I was starting to explain why I'd been at the Municipal Center and what I'd seen there when Diane burst through the back door.

"Kate, have you heard about Tim? It's all over town. Everybody's talking about it. Josie, I'm so sorry for you too. And you were so glad to have him back here." Diane swung around and threw her arms around Josie, then turned to me.

"What do you know about this, Loren? He was at your house the other night, I heard. What was that all about?"

Kate and Josie both stared at me as if they couldn't believe what they were hearing. "He was at your house? Why would he be at your house?" Kate asked

"You mean the night after we went to his place for lunch?" Josie chimed in. "He went to your house that night?"

The three of them stared at me. I couldn't think of where to begin to explain.

Diane moved closer to me. "Loren, I can't believe this. There's an ugly story making the rounds that he was at your house late and you came out to say good-bye to him in your bathrobe. Half the town thinks there's something between you and Tim."

I looked at the three angry faces staring at me, waiting for an explanation. These people were supposed to be my friends, my best friends here in Emerald Point. Was a vicious rumor all it took for them to believe the worst of me?

Tim had confided in me about his affair with Denise, but was it my place to tell his ex-wife and daughter? Right now, it looked as if Kate believed Tim had gotten involved with drugs again, and that was the reason for his arrest. And it was possible she was right. Maybe the arrest had nothing to do with Denise's murder.

Tim had worried he would be suspected, but he could have been way off base. We'd all know before long. Tomorrow's newspapers would have the story. The area radio and television stations probably had their reporters on it already. And the Post Standard would be posting tomorrow's headlines on their Internet site in a few hours.

I didn't try to explain anything. Instead, I picked up my coffee cup, swung around fast and stormed out of Kate's kitchen. As I passed Herb, I slid the cup along the counter toward him and kept going fast. By the time I got to my car, I was shaking, but I managed to stab the key into the ignition, start the engine and take off for home.

Once I reached my house—fortunately without killing myself or anybody else— I flung myself into a kitchen chair and tried to calm down. I left the outside lights on thinking that Don might come back from Albany. He hadn't called. That could mean he was on the road—or maybe it just meant he was too busy to think about letting me know his plans.

I kept listening for a car. Josie had always been able to find a million reasons to stop by, but apparently, she couldn't find even one tonight. As the evening wore on, I debated about calling Kate. I didn't think she'd come over, but maybe she'd call.

I fixed something to eat—a sandwich of some kind, I guess it was—and tossed it into the garbage after a couple of bites. I poured a glass of wine, then a second, then I guess I must have had a third because I fell asleep on the couch.

When I woke up, I staggered to my computer and clicked on the Post Standard web site. The next day's headlines were already up. Topping the news, in bold face type more appropriate for a national disaster than an area news report, came the report about the arrest of Timothy Donohue of North Road, Mountainside, as a person of interest in the investigation of Denise McNaughton's death.

No charges were listed. No details about why he was a person of interest. Just the bare facts.

I dragged myself upstairs and fell into bed. By some miracle I slept. By the time I unglued my eyelids and looked at the clock the next morning, it was after eight o'clock.

The one good thing about my ferocious hangover was that it left me mentally and physically unable to reprocess the thoughts which led to my excessive alcohol consumption in the first place. Staggering into and out of the shower without falling over demanded complete concentration; finding something to wear required my closest attention; deciding how to spend the day took every available ounce of brain power.

Since I was now devoid of both friends and fiancé, the last decision wasn't that difficult. Work loomed as the only viable alternative. Luckily for me, I had a job and it was waiting for me a few miles down the road.

A short time later, I opened my office in the Village Building, collapsed into the chair behind my desk and tried to achieve some degree of normalcy. As a first step, I consumed two large mugs of my favorite Vermont-blend coffee and made sure a fresh supply was dripping into the carafe.

Once I'd fortified myself with the coffee, I opened the copy of the Post Standard which had been tossed on the doorstep and read through the article on Tim's arrest. As far as I could remember, it was the same information I'd found last night on the paper's website. A small article on the next page mentioned that Lucas Prendergast, known as the Woodsman, the man who'd also been detained as a person of interest in Denise McNaughton's murder, had been transferred for testing to a psychiatric facility in Utica.

Did that mean Tim had been elevated to prime suspect? And what did this transfer mean for poor Luke? Neither of these things sounded like good news to me.

Pauline—God bless her—arrived a half hour later.

She tried to sound casual, but her expression was serious. "I thought I'd come in early, Loren, and see if you were here and how you were doing."

"Because you expected I might not be doing well?" No sense beating around the bush. Pauline was now the only person I could talk to.

"It's that Teddie Murray. How did she ever get herself elected? Have you heard what she's doing now?"

"I've heard some rumors." I knew whatever I'd heard, Pauline would have picked up ten times more information. It would be better to find out what she knew now and get it over with.

She settled herself in the chair beside my desk. "Loren, she started by telling everyone you were befriending the Woodsman. That was the expression she used first, befriending him. Then she switched to saying you were supporting him, trying to get him released. She even claimed you offered to have him released in your custody."

"Diane told me she heard that too. There's not one word of truth there, Pauline. I did go down to the jail to see him, went twice in fact. I'm not sure he had any idea who I was."

"This is the part I don't understand. Why did you go to see him?" She stopped and stared at me, waiting for my answer.

I recounted the story about Luke's friendship with my grandfather, how he was around a lot when I was a kid, how he was kind to me.

Pauline went on waiting. She spread her hands apart in a way that said "so, there's got to be more here than that."

I knuckled under. "He helped me out of some trouble once, Pauline."

"Trouble?"

"I was really young. I'd taken a canoe out. I wasn't supposed to use it, but I'd done it anyway. I dropped the paddles, both of them, in the water. The canoe started floating away from the dock, out into the lake, and I couldn't stop it. It might not sound like much now, but my grandfather was tough about things like that. I think he got sick of having me there, would have loved to find a reason to say I couldn't spend the rest of the summer with my grandmother. He'd already warned me: 'You tick me off one more time, missy, and you've had it. You won't be visiting us anymore.'"

"He'd have sent you home?"

"More than that. He was telling me I wouldn't be able to spend summers with them anymore."

"And that meant a lot to you?"

"Everything. It meant the world to me," I said.

Pauline gave me a questioning look, but she didn't ask for details.

"Things weren't very good for me at home."

"And Luke helped you?"

"All of a sudden, he came wading into the water. It got too deep for him to stand. I thought sure he'd stop then, but he dove in and began to swim toward me. He had all his clothes on. When he reached the canoe, he grabbed hold of it and began trying to tow it back to the dock. It seemed to take him forever, but I didn't know how to help. I could tell he was getting tired. I thought he'd have to give up, but he didn't"

Pauline listened. She didn't interrupt me or ask questions; she just listened.

I went on, "After he'd tied the canoe up to a post, he started diving for the paddles. They weren't anywhere near together. He got one, but he had to keep diving over and over until he found the other. Then he helped me up onto the dock, and the next thing I knew, he was gone. I never got a chance to thank him."

"So that's what you're doing now?"

"Maybe. I hadn't thought of it that way. Maybe that is what I'm doing now."

"You could have drowned, of course. So you're thanking him for saving your life?"

"Not just that. For not telling my grandfather."

"You mean he never told him?"

"I was terrified. I thought the next time he came over, he'd tell him what had happened and I'd never get to come to the lake again. I worried myself sick about that for weeks, but he never told on me."

Pauline stared at me in the calm, steady way she had which would force anyone to reveal the truth. Sometimes I kidded her about it, told her she should work for the sheriff, or for the F.B.I. She'd be invaluable when they wanted a culprit to confess.

"Was your life really that bad at home?" she asked finally.

"It was that bad," I said.

But, fortunately, the past was over and done with. Right now, it was my present-day life which was spiraling from bad to worse. Not only had I alienated my best friends in Emerald Point and given myself the world's worst hangover in the bargain, I'd dredged up unhappy times I'd tried hard to forget. I needed to find something else to focus my attention on.

For the last week, I'd been trying to get to a report on the proliferation of oversized summer homes, nicknamed McMansions, on the lake. The subject, which already had many Emerald Point residents steamed, was going to be a tough one to tackle. Some of the longtime residents saw the elaborate pleasure palaces being built by recent arrivals as an eyesore which totally changed the look and character of the shoreline. Like many others who lived on the lake, I wished there were a way to control this kind of growth, but right then I had no idea how that could be done.

What I couldn't stop thinking about was Denise McNaughton's murder and the way it had disrupted the peace and harmony, not only of Mountainside and Emerald Point, but of my own world as well. In my efforts to find out more about Denise's life and her possible killer, I'd consulted the regional wise women, Ramona and Pauline, chatted up two of Denise's co-workers, Bobbie and Lee, and pried what limited information I could get out of Investigator Jim Thompson. Where else could I go?

Unless I followed a time-honored tradition and killed two birds with one stone? I thought of a way I could do exactly that.

Jeannie Spenser, Ramona's daughter, had earned everyone's respect as the A Number 1, top real estate broker in the area. Jeannie, despite her soft-sounding name, was famous for her willingness to play hardball and, in the course of her real estate wheelings and dealings, she made it her practice to collect information about people in the area the rest of us never had access to. What if I chatted her up about the McMansions and their owners, then sequeled into a conversation about Denise's murder?

Prying information out of Jeannie wasn't exactly easy, but since she considered me a friend of her mother's, she sometimes gave a little. Jeannie could not only offer insights into the McMansion problem for me to bring to the next Village Board meeting, she might know the name of the man Tim suspected Denise had been seeing.

One of the advantages of being mayor, even of a town like Emerald Point, is that the position opens doors which might otherwise be closed to you. All it took was a phone call to Jeannie's office and I had an appointment that afternoon. Jeannie was "squeezing me in" her secretary told me, "and happy she was able to make herself available."

Jeannie didn't keep me waiting. She ushered me into her office—so much more elegant than mine, I immediately started thinking about redecorating—and we exchanged a few pleasantries. I didn't waste time, but plunged right into Subject #1, the increasing number of McMansions springing up around the lake.

The word was all it took to set her off. "McMansions, Loren? Yes, we all should be concerned. So many of them are not well built, and they're definitely oversized for the number of people who are going to live in them. 'wallboard palaces,' one of my colleagues calls them, and with some of them anyway, he's not far off the mark."

"Aren't there ways communities can restrict this kind of growth?" I asked her.

"Right now, they're limited in what they can do. But some builders I've talked with say people are no longer asking for the largest of these monstrosities."

Her remark surprised me. "You think the trend is moving away from them?"

"To some extent. Back in the '90's, the average size of these homes went from 1500 square feet to 2300 square feet, but recently that growth has slowed."

"But I see them going up, fortunately not in Emerald Point yet, but in other places on the lake," I said.

"Perhaps, but for the most part, not as large as a few years ago and now being built at a much slower rate," Jeannie went on. "I think you'll find, Loren, that the Gen X'ers are choosing amenities over size. Most of the couples I've worked with lately prefer quality to quantity where their homes are concerned."

"I didn't realize that." I hadn't always understood the thinking of others in my own age group. I couldn't begin to understand what was important to the new wave of Gen X'ers.

"What most of these people want now isn't so much the space, but the bells and whistles, the sub-zero refrigerators, the radiant heating, the architectural moldings. Not everyone, of course. One of my clients in your town is thinking very large, even has her heart set on a glass-walled conservatory."

"A what? Do you mean a greenhouse?"

Jeannie smiled at my question. "Of course, a greenhouse is essentially what she's talking about, but notice how much more elegant it sounds when you refer to it as a conservatory."

"With the kind of winters we have here?"

"Yes, and it's to be part of the house. No one can talk her out of it. She's the exception, though. Apparently she's wanted to build a new house for a long time. It's taken her years to convince her husband, and she's finally talked him into it. Next step: find a lot large enough so she can go all out."

"She can't build on the lake, can she? There isn't enough shoreline left in Emerald Point for a McMansion, is there?"

"If you removed an existing building, you could do it."

"But the cost... Wouldn't that be astronomical?"

"Of course. Unless the alternative came with an even higher price." Jeannie dipped her head and gave me a knowing look.

A wasted ploy on her part, since I didn't have the foggiest idea what she was implying.

Before I could begin to decode her message, she sprang up from her chair and extended her hand. "It's always good seeing you, Loren. Drop in any time."

At that point her meaning was clear, and I got it. Our meeting was over, and before I'd even brought up Denise's murder. I realized what had happened. Jeannie had told me something, something she regretted mentioning a few seconds later.

If only I could figure out what it was.

Chapter 11

When I pulled into my driveway a half hour later, Kate's Catering van was parked on the street in front of my house. As I got out of my car, Kate hurried toward me, lugging one of her watermelon-colored catering baskets. Diane followed a few steps behind balancing several grocery bags.

"We've come to apologize," Kate said, as she set down the basket and threw her arms around me, "and get back in your good graces by bringing delicious things to eat. Tell me you haven't been out to a fabulous luncheon somewhere."

"As a matter of fact, I've forgotten all about lunch."

"Perfect," Diane said. "And if you're willing to share with a couple of people who deserve failing grades on the friendship test, ask us in. We'll provide lunch and try to make it up to you."

"I'm willing." I blinked back the tears that were pricking at my eyes and hurried to unlock the door.

Once we'd shed our coats, Diane produced a bottle of wine from one of her bags. As I reached into the hutch for three wine glasses, Kate unwrapped a platter of crudités and a three-part serving dish, piled high with delicacies—one part, crabmeat dip and two parts, my personal favorite, Kate's liver paté. Nothing said I'm sorry like an extra portion of Kate's liver paté.

As soon as we'd sampled the hors d'oeuvres, Kate reached across the table and took my hand. "Loren, I hardly know where to begin. Having Tim back here has put me on edge, but that's no excuse for the way I acted."

"It's understandable," I said. "The guy has me on edge too, and I've only known him for two days. He came here the other night—I guess you've both heard that—because he thought I could help him. He was afraid he was going to be a suspect in Denise's murder."

"You'd only known him for two days and, according to local gossip, you entertained him in your night attire? That's Teddie Murray's version anyway," Diane said.

"It was a below-zero night, and my furnace couldn't cope with it. I had my heavy bathrobe on over my clothes, but I was fully dressed underneath—doesn't that count for something, Your Honor? And how would Teddie know anyway?" I said.

Kate handed me another cracker spread with pate. It was beyond delicious.

I'd devoured that one and was reaching for another when a memory bolt hit me. "Wait. I bet I can answer that question myself. When I opened the door for Tim to leave, there was a car parked across the street. It started up fast and drove away the minute he stepped outside. So take your pick. That could have been someone following Tim or someone spying on me. And if it was Teddie Murray, or one of her cohorts, that would mean she stakes out my house."

"Go back to the reason Tim came to see you. Why would the sheriff's department suspect him of killing Denise?" Kate asked me.

I was searching for a way to answer that question when Diane intervened.

"He was seeing her, Kate. I'm sorry, but that bit of gossip has been on everybody's radar this week. You mean you didn't know?"

Kate recoiled. "No, I didn't know. Do you think Josie does?"

"If she does, she hasn't let on to me," I said.

Diane believed in telling the truth even when it hurt. "Not yet maybe, Kate, but she will. So you'd better be prepared for it."

An hour later, after Kate and Diane had left, I settled myself on the couch with a cup of tea and a new Julia Spencer-Fleming mystery I thought would help me concentrate on something besides Emerald Point and the crazy goings-on in my world here. For the first time in days, I thought I could pronounce my life almost under control. The visit from Kate and Diane had changed everything. I was back on good terms with them—and hopefully, that meant Josie as well. Don had called from Albany to apologize for not getting through to me the night before and to explain that he would be gone at least one more day, maybe two.

There was one last thread to tie up—Teddie Murray. Time to beard her in her own den. I'd never known exactly how that was done, but I was ticked enough to take a stab at it.

The next morning when I arrived at the office, I put in a phone call to her.

"Teddie," I said when she came on the line, dripping sugarcoated how-was-I's. "I've been thinking about your suggestion we get together for lunch. What about today? I could pick you up about 12, if you can get clear."

I heard her startled intake of breath. "Loren?"

I'd taken her by surprise. I wasn't sure what she did when she wasn't making trouble for me, but from what she'd said at my party about having lunch, I thought she could make time when she wanted to.

She recovered fast. "Of course, Loren. I'd love to."

"I'll pick you up at noon then," I said and rang off.

"I think Mario's would be a good choice for us, don't you?" I declared two hours later when she was settled in my car. "I'm in the mood for a pizza, and I don't know a better place to get one."

I caught a quick eyebrow-raise of what I suspected was disappointment, but she didn't object. "Fine with me."

When we arrived at Mario's, we found at least three-quarters of the tables and booths occupied, some by college kids home on their winter breaks, some by people from the downtown stores and offices treating themselves to Mario's specials on their lunch hours.

Mario himself hurried over to take our order. "Good to see you, Mayor. Did you have a nice Christmas?"

"Great," I said. Stretching the truth about your Christmas was not only accepted practice here in Emerald Point, it was expected.

"Mario," Teddie said. No warmth in her voice.

Oops. Something going on there.

"Yeah. Hi, Mrs. Murray. What can I get for you ladies today?"

I didn't hesitate; I asked for a cup of coffee. This didn't seem like a good time to loosen anyone's tongue (especially mine) with the demon wine—and ordered one of Mario's individual pizzas with mushrooms.

Teddie, after a moment's hesitation, made the same choices.

"Want the coffee now?" Mario asked.

When I nodded, he signaled to Alicia Smithson, a college student working the counter on her holiday break. "We've just made a fresh pot. She'll run it right over to you."

Then there was nothing left to talk about except the serious stuff—like my impeachment maybe. Except Teddie didn't seem to know how to get that topic off the ground.

I took the initiative. "There are some really strange rumors around.

Have you heard them? Stories about the Woodsman, how I'm trying to help him. One of them has me bringing him to live with me. Do you believe this town sometimes?"

Teddie, her face growing pinker by the second, shook her head. I waited, gave her a chance to talk.

When she didn't say anything, I rambled on. "People will believe the darnedest stories. It's probably a good thing they've sent him to Utica for some testing. Maybe that will give our sheriff's department time to find the real murderer. Talk about a case of somebody being in the wrong place at the wrong time. That guy could end up with a long prison sentence because he helped himself to a couple of articles of clothing on a bitter cold night."

Teddie finally found her voice. She sounded a little shaky at first, but then her usual self-confidence kicked in. "Clothing? Oh there's more than clothing involved, a lot more."

"Really? What else? I haven't heard about anything else," I said.

"I heard there were several other things belonged to Denise McNaughton, taken right out of her house."

"I don't think so. From what I've heard, the clothes are the main thing they have against him. People have zeroed in on that anyway, and it's really very flimsy evidence. He apparently stole a few items of clothing from Denise's house, and not only from her place but a half dozen others. Of course, nobody else got murdered, so thefts from their houses hardly rate a mention."

Teddie killed some time tugging paper napkins out of Mario's overloaded dispenser and setting them at our places, but she wasn't ready to back down. "I can't understand why you're taking his side, Loren. I know people say he was a friend of your grandfather's, but that doesn't mean anything now."

Alicia delivered our pizzas and refilled our coffee cups. She created enough stir that Teddie managed to get in a follow-up crack I couldn't quite make out—something to the effect that being a friend of my grandfather's wasn't any recommendation in a lot of people's minds either. Zing,

I pretended I didn't hear her.

By the time I'd dropped Teddie off and got back to the Village Building, the pizza had solidified into a huge lump in my stomach and I'd mentally crossed Teddie off any future lunch lists. As I pulled into my parking space, I was giving serious thought to closing up shop for the day—Pauline wasn't coming in—when I saw a man I didn't recognize leaning on his car outside my office. He waved and walked over to where I'd parked.

"Can you spare me a few minutes, Mayor Graham? Doug Baxter's the name. I've got a problem I'd like to run by you."

The last thing I felt like at that point was another problem, but hey, that's why the village paid me the big bucks. "Come right on in, Mr. Baxter." I led him into my office and pointed to a chair.

Doug Baxter took a minute to settle himself and unzip his parka. He looked to be in his mid-forties, his full head of brown hair fading to gray, his face tanned and weathered as if he worked outdoors. He looked vaguely familiar, but I couldn't think where I'd seen him before.

"You helped me out a couple years ago with a zoning problem I had. Figured I could talk to you. Don't want to go to the sheriff, but need some advice."

"This sounds like a problem could be helped by coffee," I said.

When he nodded, I plugged in the pot behind my desk. I'd already fixed it with water and coffee, so it was ready to start.

"I own a share in a hunting camp up near Beaver Falls. A week or so ago my friend Brad Thomas and I took our snowmobiles up there one day, thinkin' we'd check the place out. Heard a noise upstairs and the next thing you know, this guy comes barreling down the stairs and out the front door."

He'd piqued my interest. I wanted to hear more. "Does that mean the guy was gone before you got much of a look at him?"

"At that point, but we chased him into the woods. He was limping pretty bad, so he wasn't very fast. We grabbed him and hustled him back inside the camp and asked him some questions. I didn't realize it at first, but it was that Woodsman guy, the one they picked up a couple days ago for murdering the nurse."

"Not for murdering her. They called him a person of interest," I said.

I stood up and poured two cups of coffee. I slid one of them across the desk to him, along with the sugar and powdered creamer.

"Black's fine with me. Thanks." He stopped talking long enough to take a couple of swallows.

"Then what happened?"

"Well, Mayor, he'd been staying in our place there pretty as you please. He'd built a fire—not that you could blame him for that. It was down around zero. He took some venison out of a locker we have outside and thawed it and cooked it over the fire. You could smell it—smelled damn good, I'd have to give him that. He'd found a couple of onions in the back shed that weren't frozen too bad and opened a can of tomatoes to throw in."

"You think he was staying right there in your camp?"

"Had been for a while anyway. We could see he'd slept in one of the beds, kept a fire going with the wood we had stored there and ate a couple meals anyway, maybe more."

"So? Could you talk with him at all? Did he say anything?" I was remembering Luke as he was at the jail, almost mute, not offering any explanations.

"Not at first. Thought he couldn't talk. Took a while, but then he said he didn't mean no harm, even pulled out a bunch of dirty dollar bills from a pocket and said he could pay for what he ate."

"What did you say to that?"

"You couldn't help feel sorry for the guy. I looked over at Brad, thinking he was gonna want to come down real hard on him, and he said. "No problem. We don't want your money, and it doesn't look like you did us much damage. But you probably ought to take off now."

"Was that all right with you?"

"Yeah. Especially when the guy said he had to get goin' anyway. I kinda regretted it though afterward—it was mighty cold out there—but I was worrying about him having a fire in the camp, not watching it close enough. We're really careful when we're up there. Brad and I are only part owners, you know. There'd have been hell to pay with the other guys if we'd told him to stay, and he'd managed to burn the place down. I didn't think we should speak for everybody else. Brad neither."

I didn't comment. I was seeing Luke trudging off into the bitter cold Adirondack night.

" I felt bad watchin' him leave," Doug went on, "but then I thought there'd be no reason he couldn't move back in the minute we were gone. We took off ten minutes later on our snowmobiles, and that was the last I saw of him."

"And you're telling me this because...?" I was having trouble putting my thoughts in order.

"Because this happened on the same day that broad was killed—the nurse, you know, the one's been in all the papers. Even if that guy had left right then, no way could he have got all the way down to Mountainside and killed her, even late that night. No way."

"So your statement will clear him then. This is good of you to come forward like this. If you want me to, I can go with you right now to Jim Thompson—he's the Sheriff's Department Investigator handling the case—and you can tell him what you just told me."

"No can do, Mayor. I tried to make that clear."

I thought back to the beginning of our conversation. "Did you say there was some reason you didn't want to go to the sheriff?"

"Got some issues, let's say. Like jackin' some deer maybe. Other problems."

"What about your friend? What did you say his name was?"

"Didn't say. He feels the same way I do—even more."

"But it's really important that you report this."

"Yeah. I know. That guy may not have much, but at least he's not in prison. That's why I'm tellin' you. I figure you can handle it for me. But if my name gets brought up, I'd have to deny the whole story."

"But…" My mind was racing. I struggled for a way to persuade him to talk to Jim or anybody else at the sheriff's department. The words didn't come.

"Thanks for the coffee." He got to his feet fast, gave me a thumbs up and swung out the door as he was zipping his jacket.

Damn. No way would Jim Thompson appreciate getting this information from me. But maybe I could get a temporary reprieve. This was New Year's Eve. Even Jim would take off early, and the Municipal Center offices should be closed tomorrow. Two days. Maybe that would give me time to confirm Doug's story. He had mentioned his buddy's name and I remembered what it was—Brad Thomas.

Chapter 12

I made a quick check of the telephone book when I got home, but there was no Brad Thomas listed. I was on my way to the computer to see if I could turn him up, when Don walked in the door and enveloped me in a hug.

"What would you like to do to usher in the New Year?" he said. "We could drive up to Bolton Landing and spend a fabulous night dining and dancing at the Sagamore Hotel. We could even get a room there and stay overnight in a romantic setting. I could make up for my absence that way."

"That sounds like something I'd hate to pass up. But wouldn't it be very expensive, especially after you've already bought me the beautiful necklace?"

He nodded. "Scandalously. So much so I'm counting on you to refuse the invitation."

"Okay then. I refuse. How about pizza at Mario's?"

"Perfect. My kind of night," he said.

"Mine too," I said.

We couldn't have been more wrong.

When Don pulled up in front of Mario's Pizzeria that evening, we got our first clue that something out of the ordinary was going on in downtown Emerald Point. Cars, trucks, suburbans, motorcycles, even snowmobiles lined both sides of Main Street. The parking lots and the driveways of the houses near the business district were filled.

"What the heck's going on?" Don asked

"I forgot about this. The PTA is sponsoring a special teen night for New Year's Eve. Got permission to use the old movie theatre for one night, show a couple of classic movies and have a band and dancing for the kids," I said.

"All at the same time?"

I poked him hard in the arm. "Film in the theater, dancing in the old bus garage out back. No alcohol. I thought it sounded like a good idea, although I didn't expect it to draw this much of a crowd."

"Do you want to stop in?"

"Let's just see how things are going."

"You go on in then. I'll find a place to park and meet you inside in five minutes—or ten if I'm unlucky."

The lobby of the theater—at one time the village's star attraction—had suffered with the passing years. The murals of the lake and mountains, which the town fathers had commissioned years before from a respected Adirondack painter, had faded, chipped and blurred into a dull hodgepodge of color.

Josie Donohue, standing with other teenagers near the closed ticket window, waved and yelled when she spotted me. She squeezed through the crowd to where I was standing. "Lor, what are you doing here?"

"Checking out the action. This seems to be the liveliest place in town. You?"

"I'm really just putting in an appearance. But be sure to tell my mother you saw me. Do you believe the size of this crowd?" She ducked her head up and then to the side in what I realized was some kind of coded message. Unfortunately, I couldn't decipher the code.

I leaned closer to her and whispered. "I know you're trying to tell me something, but I don't get it."

The head bobbing increased.

I still didn't get it. I shrugged and made a questioning face.

She dropped her voice to an almost inaudible level. "Over there. Dr. and Mrs. Kennison. They're chaperones. Isn't that rich?"

"Because?"

"You know. Remember what I told you about seeing him at Gore? Now, all of a sudden, he's the devoted husband, and he's checking out other people's behavior."

"I'm still not with you on this. All I saw him do at Gore was act like he was having a good time skiing.—just like everyone else there."

"You didn't see who he was with?"

I shook my head.

"Later, Lor. Tell you later. Remember you saw me here, and I was on my best behavior."

She melted back into the crowd and disappeared.

I'd had enough myself. I left the theater and waited for Don on the sidewalk outside. He was shaking his head and grumbling as he reached me. "We might as well have walked from your place, I'm parked that far from here."

"There's a crowd of teenagers inside the theater and more out back, I guess. Not our kind of party," I said.

We headed arm in arm toward Mario's, picking our way around ice patches, snow piles and more teenagers rushing to get to the movie or the dance. Once inside the restaurant, we encountered another mob scene. Both the dining area and the bar were packed, but we lucked out when a couple got up from two seats at the bar, and we managed to slide onto their stools.

Alicia Smithson, who I recognized from my lunch with Teddie Murray, appeared to be serving as official bartender for the evening—quite a promotion, I thought, but she was managing well.

I ordered a glass of wine, Don asked for a Coors, and we settled down for what should have been a quiet conversation. No way could we hear one another. After several false starts at small talk, we gave up and stared into the mirror behind the bar. The best we could manage was an occasional exchange of pleasantries with friends and neighbors, who squeezed behind us on their way in or out of the restaurant.

Somebody behind me tapped my arm. "Hey, Mayor," a gruff voice said in my ear, "hear you're going to bat for that Woodsman fellow. Now why would you do a stupid thing like that, I wonder."

I swiveled around a quarter turn—all I had room for—and found Burt Nichols leering at me. He reeked of beer, garlic and tobacco, not an appealing combination at best, and in the close confines of Mario's bar especially repulsive. "Bug off, Burt. Give me a call in a couple of days after I get back to work, if you want to talk."

"I'm a taxpayer in this damn town, and if I ask you a goddamn question, you're supposed to give me a goddamn answer."

What happened next happened almost too fast to keep track of. Burt threw in a couple of unattractive comments about me, my grandfather and my capabilities as a mayor—none of which were to his liking,

I advised him to bug off again, this time I admit with a little more force, and poked my elbow into his gut.

Burt uttered another curse, this one somewhat more colorful.

Don swung around on his stool and stood up. Burt, surprised to have someone invade his space, gave him a shove. "Lay off, jerk. I'm talkin' to the mayor here."

One, or maybe both of them, moved fast, and the next thing I knew Burt reared back and threw a punch at Don. Don stared at him in astonishment for a few seconds, then retaliated with a punch of his own that knocked Burt off his feet and sent him sprawling onto the floor. Luckily, people behind us managed to get out of the way, and no one else went down.

"We're out of here," I said to Don. I snatched up my coat, muttered a "sorry" at Alicia and pulled him through the crowd. We'd made it out the door and onto the sidewalk in seconds.

"Let's get to your car fast, before he decides to follow us," I said.

To my relief, Don didn't argue the point. We hurried back past the theater and cut through an alley to the parking lot where Don had left the car. Neither one of us said anything as we drove back to my house.

"Okay. Here's my best thinking," I said as we walked into the kitchen.

Don didn't answer.

I didn't let that stop me. "We turn on the television and have a relaxing drink. I unfreeze a pizza—which we probably would have ordered at Mario's anyway—and we don't talk about what happened. We watch the ball drop at Times Square and put everything else out of our minds."

Don yanked off his coat and tossed it over a chair. "So that works for tonight maybe. What about tomorrow and the day after that?"

"Tomorrow's a brand new year, a chance for a fresh start. Everything will be different then," I said.

"Is that what you think, Loren? Do you really think things will ever be any different?"

That was all he said, but his words started one of those arguments people have where nobody says anything, but accusations churn around in their heads with enough power to short circuit a brain imaging machine. At least, I assumed other couples besides Don and I had them.

I turned on the television, handed the remote to him and made tracks for the kitchen. I mixed Manhattans in a deadly combination of Canadian Club and vermouth, filled two of my best crystal glasses, shook an elegant mixture of salted nuts into a pretty little scalloped dish and slid a frozen pizza topped with hot sausage into the microwave. I doubted if even Mario himself could have come up with a more lethal combination.

I didn't have to ask Don why he was angry. He'd made it perfectly clear on other occasions that he hated to see me involved in what he usually referred to as sheriff's department business. And that's how he thought of it—the sheriff's business, not mine. I didn't get any special pass for being the mayor here or for being in a position to know more about what went on in Emerald Point than most people. If I wanted to stick my neck out—after he'd made it clear he didn't approve—that was bad enough. But when he was forced to come to my defense in a barroom brawl at Mario's on the busiest night of the year in front of half the town, matters spiraled from bad to worse.

Add to that, the fact he'd hit someone, had punched another human being in anger. Don Morrison, the quiet, reasonable, scientific type of guy who helped solve other people's problems, didn't do things like that. At least he wouldn't have—I suspected he was thinking—if I hadn't managed to drive him to it.

I handed him his drink and he downed it fast, too fast for something that lethal. When I brought in the pizza a few minutes later, he ignored the plate I set down on the small table next to him and went to the kitchen to fix himself another drink.

I didn't comment on the refill or suggest his hand might need attention or ask how things had gone in Albany. I knew all those questions were fraught with danger. Instead, I drank my drink and picked the sausages off my share of the pizza and tried to concentrate on the Boston Pops Orchestra bidding the old year farewell and welcoming the new year in, as if they actually believed that would change anything in this sorry world.

As for my own role in the evening and the days preceding it, I couldn't think how I might have averted the problem. I'd felt right about supporting the Woodsman to begin with and now, after my conversation with Doug Baxter, I was even more convinced he was innocent of Denise McNaughton's murder. So what if others didn't think so? So what if idiots like Teddie Murray insisted on making trouble. Sooner or later they'd find out they were wrong. And if I could locate Brad Thomas and get him to confirm seeing the Woodsman on the day of the murder, maybe I could help make it sooner.

By the time the ball dropped in Times Square, Don's guttural snores were drowning out the TV. I didn't try to wake him. Instead, I brought down a couple of heavy blankets to throw over him and went back upstairs. When I sat down at the window for my nightly fix of staring at the lake, the dark water, now edged with a delicate necklace of ice, stretched away from me as cold and dismal as my thoughts, and the wretched little lights along the opposite shore, which sometimes glowed like cheerful beacons, barely penetrated the gloom.

New Year's Day, in contrast, arrived as bright and shiny as a new penny. Cold, yes, but with sunlight glistening on the water in a way which made the lake—still a long way from frozen—sparkle like molten glass, and offered a refreshing contrast to the dreary atmosphere of the night before.

One way of determining that your life has come to a sorry state is to realize you have a day off and are toying with the idea of going into work. Or even worse, when you find yourself actually considering a drive down to Lake George Village to watch something called the annual Polar Bear Plunge, in which hundreds of supposedly sane men, women and adolescents rush to the beach in below freezing temperatures to wade, dive and eventually submerge themselves in the icy water.

I tiptoed by Don, still asleep on the couch, closed the door to the kitchen and made a big pot of coffee. I'd planned on serving him a couple of New Year's breakfast treats, including fresh-baked croissants and a delicious currant jelly Kate was promoting. Instead, I took a certain satisfaction in wolfing the treats down all by myself, hunched over the Post Standard, which had been delivered to my doorstep in the pre-dawn hours. Fortunately, the fight at Mario's had happened too late for the New Year's Day edition of the paper.

At nine o'clock, Josie Donohue knocked once on the outside door, yelled my name and bounded into the kitchen. "Good, Lor. You're up. How about you give me a ride to the Village, wait for me half an hour or so and then take me to Gore to meet some of the gang. Once you're there, you can see for yourself what Dr. Kennison is up to. You won't have to take my word for it."

"Slow down a minute. How did you get here? Don't you have your mother's car?" I asked her.

"Yes, but she needs it herself. If you follow me back to my house, I'll drop it off and you can run me down to the Village and check out First Day. That's another name for the Polar Bear Plunge. I won't take long there. You don't mind, do you, Lor? Otherwise, my day's down the toilet."

I sympathized with her dilemma, since my day had a pretty good start in that direction itself. "I guess I can do that. Is there something special going on in the Village?"

"Lor, I told you. I'm doing the Plunge."

My last swallow of coffee went down the wrong way and almost choked me to death. The Polar Bear Plunge had been the Lake George Village signature New Year's Day event for some years now and, for reasons far beyond my comprehension, it became more popular every year.

"You can't be serious," I gasped between coughs.

"I'm sure I mentioned it, Lor. I need to get down there."

I did more sputtering and coughing before I recovered enough to get out anything more. "You certainly did not tell me. Why, why would you do such a thing?"

"Lor, it's fun. They're gonna get over 800 people this year, they think."

"Over 800 crazies, you mean. Why would you even consider it?"

"It's the thrill of it, Lor. Plus it's a perfect way to start a new year. You wash away all the sins of the past year and start fresh. Tabula rasa, as we say in English class."

I wasn't sure what shocked me more—the idea that anyone in her right mind would dive into the frigid waters of Lake George on a ferociously cold day or the fact that a seventeen-year-old scatterbrain had spoken to me in Latin. I grabbed my heaviest parka and a wool cap out of the closet. "Okay, I'm in."

Chapter 13

I left a note for Don explaining that I was giving Josie a ride. I didn't add details about where, or make a stab at the time I'd be back. For all I knew, he'd still be asleep when I got home anyway.

As was often the case with Josie, even when her thinking appeared most off the wall, her plans fell quickly into place. I followed her home; she dropped off Kate's car, transferred her skis and a bag of beach paraphernalia into mine and we took off for Lake George Village.

To me, a plunge into the lake's icy waters might seem like a crazy idea, but apparently many, many others did not share my opinion. The streets were jammed with cars, and people of all ages crowded the sidewalks leading to Shepard's Park, located near the center of the village. The traffic had almost reached gridlock, heavier than I'd seen it on some beautiful summer days.

I let Josie off at what she assured me was the sign-up booth and drove around until I found a place to park my car. The cold was brutal. By the time I'd jogged back to the beach, I was shivering, even in a parka, hat and boots.

Despite the cold, I had to admit it was a perfect winter day. Sunlight danced across the water, and the lake beckoned, clear and welcoming—that is if one ignored the ice patches near the shore.

Josie, when I spotted her in the crowd, stood wrapped in a big yellow beach towel, waiting for the event to start.

"Lor, over here," she called.

When I reached her, I saw her only visible article of clothing besides the towel was a pair of outsized sunglasses pushed back on her head and flip flops.

"Does your mother know you're doing this?" I said as I approached her, reduced to words and tone I've always sworn I'd never use with a young person no matter what the circumstances.

"Sort of, I guess. Good news, Lor. They've got such a big crowd this year they've had to schedule two Plunges. I'm gonna be in the first one. I just made the cut."

"This is insane, you know." I couldn't seem to let up, even though almost everyone around me was in bathing attire, and I realized my thinking on the event placed me squarely in the minority.

Some of the participants had wrapped themselves in beach robes or towels. The most sensible—or cowardly, depending on your viewpoint—wore coats or parkas with only their heads and bare legs sticking out. Others had donned costumes or funny hats. Some carried toy polar bears. A hardy few—men and women both—paraded through the crowd, wearing only their bathing suits.

Josie gave me a nudge. "Hold my towel for me, will you, Lor? They say it's better to strip down beforehand and get used to the air before you go in the water."

Before I could react, Josie whipped off her towel and shoved it at me. She was now braving the elements in what I would describe as an itsy bitsy teeny weeny yellow bikini. Although many of the Plungers had obviously failed to diet or work out sufficiently before their unveilings, I had to admit Josie looked great.

A horn sounded. The first contingent of Polar Bears, Josie among them, headed for the water. Some dashed forward, hooting and hollering, splashing one another, as if refusing to acknowledge the cold. Others hung back, torturing themselves by getting wet slowly. A few of the bravest dove under water at once, at the risk, I thought, of shocking themselves to death. Parents, who I guessed were trying to set an example of courage, waded into the water hand in hand with their children, most of them I was glad to see old enough to have made their own decisions to participate.

Within minutes, the least hardy of the Plungers turned around and staggered back onto the beach. As they hurried to pick up the towels or clothing they'd tossed aside, several women moved through the crowd, carrying trays of hot chocolate and handing foam cups of it to anyone who wanted one.

I heard someone call my name.

Jane Kennison and Alice Simmons, both warmly dressed in heavy parkas, hats and scarves, came toward me, swinging empty trays.

"You've been doing a good deed. What a great idea," I said.

"Our women's group decided we'd do this as a public service," Jane said, "even though I personally think these people are insane."

"Finally, a voice of reason. I'm so glad to hear you say that. I've been wondering if I'm the crazy one, and trying to come to terms with it," I said.

"Did you plan to take part in this yourself, Loren, and then decide against it?" Alice asked me.

"Do you mean, did I come here to plunge and then chicken out? No, I brought Josie Donohue, and I'm waiting for her to come out of the water. She went with the first contingent, but I don't see her now."

"You mean her mother let her do this?" Alice went on.

"I don't know how to answer that. I just heard this morning she was going to do it," I said.

"I can't imagine Kate agreeing to something so crazy," Jane said.

"Neither can I," I said, and was saved from further comment when Josie came dashing up the beach toward us.

"Hey, you guys, it's awesome, really awesome, and it's not too late. There's room in the second wave if any of you want to join in."

"If I'd only brought my suit," I said, even though I knew sarcasm was usually lost on my young friend.

"Next year, Lor. We'll do it together. Give me five minutes in the locker room and I'll be ready to hit the slopes."

Jane and Alice shook their heads as they watched her go. If I hadn't thought it disloyal, I would have shaken mine too.

Fifteen minutes later, Josie, with the remarkable resilience of the young, was dry, dressed in her ski clothes and ready to go.

Not that the festivities were quieting down. The beach teemed with the second wave of Polar Bears, and we could hear the band tuning up at a nearby bistro in preparation for the After-Plunge party.

"You're certainly managing a full sports schedule today," I told Josie as we drove north through the Village.

"Sure, if you're gonna live in this part of the world, you gotta take part in what it has to offer," she said.

The remark brought me up short. Lately it seemed as if more and more of Josie's comments were making sense. Did this mean I should worry about myself?

We exited the Northway at Warrensburgh, followed the short-cut along the river and emerged onto 28. From then on, it was smooth sailing—driving that is—since most of the skiers heading for Gore had already reached there, and it was too early for the crowds to start leaving on their return trips.

Josie planned my visit for me. "What you want to do when we get there, Lor, is go in the restaurant and have coffee or another breakfast or something. If you sit near the windows, you can see the trails. You won't have to wait very long before you'll spot the doctor and his lady love. I'd bet money he'll be there today while his wife is tied up working the Plunge."

"Tell me who the other woman is. Don't keep me in suspense."

"I don't know her name. I've seen her around. I think she might work at the hospital too, but I'm not sure. That's your job to find out."

"So he's brought her to Gore other times?"

"Christmas Day was the first time I saw them there. He was slobbering all over her. And his wife was at our house saying how he was working the church breakfast."

"Once? That was it?"

"No. My friends tell me they were there skiing together almost every day last week."

"How can that be? Don't these people have jobs to go to?" I said.

"Lor, when the skiing's good, that's when you gotta take the days. It's supposed to warm up and rain next week."

So what did I know? I always said after I moved to this part of the world, I'd learn to ski, but I hadn't done it yet.

After Josie had fastened on her skis and taken off for more exciting activities, I sauntered into the restaurant. At the counter I ordered a cup of coffee and some kind of sweet roll which looked as if it would push any already clogged arteries over the edge in nothing flat. Undaunted, I carried it to one of the tables on the window wall and settled down to study the slopes.

The view was spectacular. The mountain, generously endowed with snow—powder I supposed was the correct term—was outlined against a sky so drenched with light I had to shield my eyes to look up at it. And the trails—there seemed to be dozens of them—were beautifully groomed and dotted with skiers swooping down them at what seemed to me death-defying speeds. Clusters of them in brightly colored ski wear mingled at the bottom. Then in a mass exodus, they hurried back to the gondolas and lifts as most opted for another run.

People appeared to be enjoying themselves—I had to give them that. Adults of all ages, teenagers, even small children seemed to know exactly what they were doing. Some headed to the lifts the minute they'd completed their downhill run. Others stood staring up the mountain, apparently keeping an eye out for friends or family members to follow them down the slopes. Parents of the youngest children waited for them at the bottom of the kiddie hill, then guided them back to the patient instructor, so they could take off for another run themselves.

I was so intent on what was going on outside I might have missed Dr. Kennison's entrance, if he hadn't made that all but impossible. He swung through the door, stomping his feet and flailing his arms as if he were close to freezing to death. The young woman who followed him into the restaurant ducked her head, apparently embarrassed by his antics. When I got a good look at her, I realized she was probably the girl Josie had spoken of. She was hanging back, keeping a few steps behind him as if embarrassed. That may have been the reason Josie hadn't realized they were together.

When she pulled off her blue ski cap and I saw her face, I recognized her—Marcie Fellows, an Emerald Point girl, who worked in the billing office at the Glens Falls Hospital. I'd gone in to talk with her once when I had a problem with a bill. She'd been pleasant enough, not a world beater in either looks or personality I didn't think, but agreeable and willing to help me with my bill.

Was this the big romance people were talking about? Marcie Fellows couldn't be more than twenty-five, too young for Ed Kennison, and she was—to put it kindly—a plain girl, shy, with nothing about her to attract a man with a supposedly roving eye.

But, of course, that was my opinion, and what did I know? My own romance had taken some hard hits last night, and I wasn't out of the woods yet. Why should I assume knowing how to keep a man happy was my forte? Right now, I had no idea what would be waiting for me when I got home.

An audible whisper from the next table caught my attention. "Yes, yes. We see you, Eddie. You can knock it off now."

I turned to see who'd spoken. Two young women in elegant ski wear were staring at Dr. Kennison and commenting on his performance. And he did seem to be playing to the gallery. He made a production of helping Marcie off with her parka, seated her at one of the tables, then gestured to a waitress that they wanted to order.

The teenage girl, handling their section, ambled over to them. "Today's special is creamed chicken on biscuits. Do you want a drink first?" Not exactly five-star service.

A noisy crowd of skiers burst through the outside doors, stomping their feet and complimenting each other on their great runs. "Let's hurry up and eat so we can get back out there. These are the best conditions so far this year," someone said.

The group found a table, actually two tables which the men pushed together with much noise and laughter. Four—no five—couples, probably in their thirties, all apparently happy, eyes sparkling, cheeks flushed from the cold. I watched them settle in, enjoying the day and one another.

By the time I turned back to where Dr. Kennison and Marcie were seated, I was surprised to find their table was empty. They were gone.

And with them went my excuse for hanging around at Gore Mountain. I could have killed another half hour or more keeping an eye on what they were doing, but now I had no reason to put off the inevitable. It was time to go home and face the music with Don. I already knew what the major hurdle would be: I didn't feel I should be blamed for what had happened at Mario's, and I was reasonably sure Don felt the incident had been all my fault.

So what was I doing here spying on a couple of people who were obviously messing up their own lives, when I needed to go home and smooth things over with a guy who'd brought good things into my own? It was New Year's after all, a time for fresh starts, new beginnings. Don and I could definitely use one.

I left a tip, paid my bill at the cashier's station and headed for the door, intending to go home and concentrate on straightening out my life.

A quick stop in the ladies' room and my good resolves went flying. Marcie Fellows stood just inside the door, her face streaked with tears, her entire body shaking with sobs.

"What's wrong? Can I do something to help?" I said.

She lifted her head and stared into the mirror. "You can't help. Nobody can help." Those few words set off a fresh flood of tears with some hiccups thrown in.

"It's New Year's. This is a day for fresh starts." I unconsciously echoed my own thoughts.

"If only that were true," she said. She waved her hand in front of the dispenser on the wall next to her until a towel came rolling out. She ripped it off, wet it and applied it to her face in a futile effort to repair some of the damage.

"I don't think there should be if only's on New Year's. This is the day for new beginnings, a day when you can start over and go after anything you want." I made this pronouncement despite the fact I had no idea why she was crying or what I was talking about.

Except I knew I wasn't being totally honest. Her distress must have something to do with the doctor, didn't it?

She dug a compact and lipstick out of her purse and made a stab at repairing her makeup, then pulled open the door. "Thanks. I know you mean well, but you have no idea what you're talking about."

"Story of my life," I said to her departing back.

By the time I tiptoed into my own kitchen a short time later, I'd thought of a half-dozen ways to open the conversation with Don. I was planning to pick one and go with it, but when I saw him sitting at the table, looking more dejected than I'd ever seen him before, I ran out of steam fast.

I leaned down and put my arms around him. "We didn't start the new year off very well, did we? I know you're not the barroom brawl type, but you were incredibly heroic and defended my honor like a medieval knight. So thank you."

"If I'd only brought my lance with me, my knuckles would hurt less today, that's for sure." He extended his right hand to show an ugly red bruise across the backs of his fingers.

I rummaged in the freezer door until I found an ice pack and wrapped it in a clean dish towel. "Put this on it for a few minutes. They swear it helps."

To my surprise, he accepted the pack and settled it on his hand. "I don't know how you put up with those characters. That guy was an idiot. Who is he anyway?" he said.

"Burt Nichols. He has a reputation as a really bad drunk, and it's easy to see how he earned it," I said.

"It's well deserved, that's for sure."

I started coffee as I waited for the other shoe to drop, but Don didn't say anything more.

So I rattled on. "You may have convinced him to lay off me. Sometimes with guys like that, calling their bluff is all it takes."

"I wouldn't count on it, but I hope you're right. Where did you go earlier?"

That was the best question he could have asked because it swung the subject around to the Winter Carnival and Josie's participation in the Polar Bear Plunge. When Don acted interested, I told him more about the event which we both agreed was loaded with local color and merited a chuckle or two.

"And guess who was playing Good Samaritan handing out hot cocoa to the plungers."

Before I could fill him in on Jane and Alice and their hot chocolate distribution, or even touch on the trip to Gore and the appearance of Jane's husband with his young friend, we heard a car pull up outside.

"Now what?" Don said.

Someone knocked lightly on the back door. I opened it to find Tim Donohue, looking only marginally better than when I'd seen him in the back of the sheriff's car.

"Loren, I'm sorry to bother you again, but can I talk to you?"

"Sure," I said with a little more good cheer than I had to spare. "Come in and sit down. Do you know Don Morrison?"

The men exchanged hellos. Don didn't offer to shake hands or explain about the ice pack.

As I poured Tim a cup of coffee, I asked him, "When I saw you in the sheriff's car, I was afraid you were headed for jail. Did they decide not to charge you?"

Don looked startled by my question, so I suggested Tim fill us in on what had happened both before and after I'd seen him at the Municipal Center.

Tim swallowed several mouthfuls of his coffee. "Those sheriff's deputies—two of them—drove up to my house and started asking me questions about my relationship with Denise McNaughton. I got a little ornery, I guess, especially when they suggested taking me down to the Municipal Center. I didn't see why they couldn't ask me what they wanted to know right there at my house. Anyway I lost my cool and the next thing I knew, they'd handcuffed me and shoved me into the back of their car."

"So what was your relationship to her?" Don asked him. Don wasn't a beat-around-the-bush kind of guy at any time, especially today.

Tim gave him his stock answer. "I was seeing her."

"Does that mean you were sleeping with her?" Don asked. Curt and to the point.

"Okay. Yes. But I wasn't the only one. She had another guy, at least one. Like I told Loren, I thought she was breaking up with him, but I don't know who he was."

Don glanced over at me. I didn't like the look. "Like you told Loren? What would she have to do with it?"

I had the good sense not to utter a word.

Tim, realizing he'd blundered, tried to smooth things over. "Josie wanted me to meet Loren. She thinks the world of her, and I thought maybe she could help me out with this Denise thing. I only came back here a few weeks ago and I'm already in the hot seat in a murder investigation. I could end up going to jail."

"You think Loren could prevent that?"

"Nah, I don't mean that. But I thought Loren might know who else Denise was seeing. I had the idea she was going to break up with somebody she'd been going with and I'm thinkin' that's the guy who killed her. But I don't know who it was."

Tim's explanation sounded logical enough—at least it did to me—so I waited for Don to digest his story. It took a minute.

"So how do you stand now with the sheriff's department? Do you have an alibi for when Denise was killed?" he asked Tim.

I held my breath, expecting him to tell Don what he'd confided in me about the night of the murder.

He kept his answer short. "Not a very good one, but I didn't kill her. I swear it."

"What about that Woodsman guy? I thought they had him pegged as the murderer?" Don said.

Once again, I let Tim do the answering.

"They've sent him off to Utica for some testing. Doesn't sound as if they have enough to accuse him right now," Tim said.

"Well, at least they haven't arrested you. That's a good sign, isn't it?"

"Yeah, I guess." Tim got to his feet.

"If I hear anything, I'll let you know," I said. I couldn't think of anything else I could offer to do for him.

He handed me a piece of paper with a telephone number written on it. "I was hoping you'd say that, Loren. I realize I'm turning into a pest, but I don't know anybody else who can help me. If you hear anything more, I wish you'd give me a call."

I shoved the paper into my pocket. I had to admit I didn't mind seeing him go. I could tell Don was ready for some peace and quiet, and the truth of the matter was, so was I.

Chapter 14

The next morning, after Don had left for another couple of days in Albany, the questions about the murder which I'd been trying to ignore surfaced again and started churning around in my head. At this time Tim, the Woodsman and this unnamed stranger Denise was supposedly seeing appeared to be the obvious suspects, but they couldn't be the only ones. Denise had been linked to a number of men, besides her ex-husbands. There had to be other suspects, and by now the sheriff's department would probably have found out who they were.

I thought back to what Investigator Thompson had said. "Mayor, I'm not ready to discuss this case with you yet." Wasn't that the way he'd put it? Yet. Didn't that imply he would be ready to discuss the case with me at a later date? Maybe this would be a good day to take a ride down to his office.

One thing I'd learned about gleaning information from Jim was that the best approach required careful priming of the pump. If I could go in acting as if I already had some knowledge of the subject at hand, I'd find out a lot more than if I arrived, hat in hand, hoping he'd supply all the information.

I knew exactly where to go for help. Plus I had a good idea on how to bring up the subject. I put in a call to Stephanie Colvin, Features Editor of the Post Standard and a longtime friend.

"Stephanie," I said when she picked up her phone, "calling to wish you a happy New Year and remind you we talked about a feature on Emerald Point's plans for the year ahead. We had our best holiday season ever, according to our downtown merchants, and we want to keep that ball rolling. I've got some facts and figures on our new incentives I want to give you. I think they'll be just what you need if you want to do a story on our efforts."

"Loren, you never cease to amaze me. When they told me you were on the line, I thought you might want me to squelch a report we got about your friend Don Morrison engaging in some New Year's Eve fisticuffs."

Oops. Why did I think that was going away? "You didn't have anything about that on the Post Standard web page last night, Stephanie, or in today's paper, so I thought maybe you guys would cut us a break and not use it."

"I wish, Loren. You know if it was up to me, we wouldn't, but there are those who think it's news, and we can't pretend it didn't happen."

Actually, that was exactly what Don and I had been trying to do—pretend it didn't happen—but I decided not to share that tidbit with Stephanie. Instead, I dusted off my standard explanation. "The guy was drunk and obnoxious to me and took a swing at Don. Don hit him back. In the best of all possible worlds, it could be swept under the mat. But your editor's gotta do what he's gotta do. I really called to talk to you about something else."

Stephanie didn't press me for details on what I had on my mind, but agreed to meet me for coffee at Pappy's Restaurant a block from the Post Standard office. An hour later I was settled in and, since it was lunch time by then, treating myself to one of the restaurant's famous Pappy Burgers.

Stephanie rushed in ten minutes late—not her usual practice. With her black wool coat partly unbuttoned, her green print Hermes scarf dangling and her blonde hair wind-tossed, she was the picture of a well-dressed, but harried newspaper reporter on assignment.

"Sorry to be late," she said as she tumbled into the booth across from me. "I really have been meaning to call you. There's a lot more news coming out of your part of the world than a barroom brawl. We may have to send a reporter up there full time, what with the murder and the McMansion controversy flaring up again. What have you got for me today?"

"As promised—some facts and figures about our successful holiday season." I handed her an envelope of newsworthy items—all positive—about Emerald Point.

She slid my offering into her briefcase. "Good. Give me until next week anyway, and I'll call you to discuss this."

She'd opened another door, and I was more than willing to go through it. "As for the McMansions, I'd love to get your views on them, but right now I'm more concerned with the murder. And may I point out—the murder didn't take place in Emerald Point, remember. Mountainside has to get the credit. I'd like to find out what you're hearing at the paper. Jim gave me his 'not ready to discuss it' line."

Stephanie signaled to a waitress and asked for coffee. "As I'm sure you're aware, Loren, they suspected that guy they call the Woodsman, maybe still do suspect him, but apparently for some reason they're not willing to charge him."

I hesitated, then plunged in. "One possibility, as I understand it, is that he might have been too far away even to get to Denise's house at the time of the murder. I heard a couple of hunters saw him fifteen or more miles up in the mountains late that same day. No vehicle, no way to get to Mountainside."

"Anybody you can name?" Stephanie asked.

"Only off the record. Did you ever hear of a guy named Doug Baxter?"

"Unfortunately yes. From what I've heard about him, he's not exactly a guy you'd want to count on too heavily."

"That seems to be part of the problem. I heard yesterday that he and a friend of his could give the Woodsman an alibi, but they don't want to go to the sheriff," I said.

"What about this other guy they questioned, Tim Donohue? Don't tell me he's some relative of your friend Kate? To me, it sounds like he might be the one who killed her."

That wasn't an observation I wanted to hear. "I don't want to think either of the suspects they're looking at now killed her. You're right. Tim is Kate's ex-husband, Josie's father. He came back here recently, says he's trying to make up to Josie for the years he's been gone."

"Like that's going to be easy," Stephanie said.

"And the Woodsman—Lucas Prendergast is the name, but he also goes by Luke Prenders—was a friend of my grandfather's, did me a big favor when I was a kid, practically saved my life. Since I don't see either of them as the murderer, I'm hoping the sheriff's department's going to come up with other suspects."

Stephanie set her coffee cup down with a clatter. "Loren, I thought you weren't going to get involved in stuff like this. Didn't you tell me that the last time we talked?"

"Yes, but here I am again. It just happens somehow. I'm on my way now to talk to Investigator Thompson. He's sometimes reluctant to tell what he knows, so I need to go in with as much information as I can get ahead of time. Sort of prime the pump."

"Well, you probably know this already—Denise McNaughton had

a number of men in her life, one or more of them may have been married. So right away you can come up with several different scenarios. Maybe a guy's so crazy about her he can't stand sharing her and kills her. Or a woman finds out Denise is messing with her husband and she kills her for that. Or maybe it's the other way around—the man kills her when she threatens to tell his wife about their affair. Take your pick."

"Jim seemed to suspect it was man, I guess. Maybe thought the killing was too violent for a woman," I said.

Stephanie caught our waitress's eye and held up her coffee cup. "Isn't that thinking a little sexist now that more women are working out, getting themselves in tiptop shape?"

"I suppose," I said. "I don't much care if the killer's male or female as long as the sheriff comes up with more suspects."

"I can't help you there, Loren. I don't have any inside information on who killed Denise or why. Now the McMansion story—that's got everybody talking."

"Even here in Glens Falls?" I asked.

"Sure. The latest news is that Ed and Jane Kennison have bought some lakefront property next to their own place with plans to do a tear-down and build new and very large."

"Build a McMansion, you mean?" I said.

"The doctor's creating a lot of gossip these days. He's dating some young thing from the hospital, being very obvious about it. Takes her skiing or to dinner somewhere every chance he gets. In the meantime, Jane's dickering for the property up there. One theory is the girlfriend's the price she's gotta pay for him going along with the bigger and better house."

I nodded. "So you're saying people are talking, not just about the romance, but about the way he's flaunting it?"

Stephanie drained her second cup of coffee. "I'm saying, big house, big price. Maybe bigger than we know. Maybe a hellavu lot bigger than we'd even suspect."

Later that afternoon, I sat down across from Sheriff's Investigator Jim Thompson in his office, hoping to find out more about the investigation into Denise McNaughton's murder.

I thought opening our conversation with a sympathetic remark about the timing of the murder might get us off to a good start. "Jim, did your New Year's turn out any better than your Christmas?"

He tried to keep a straight face, but didn't quite manage it. "Turned out better than some people's, I guess. At least I didn't end up in a barroom brawl."

Sympathy wasted. I should have known better. "Occupational hazard sometimes in Emerald Point. I was hoping that news wouldn't get spread around."

"I bet Morrison's not too happy about it. He doesn't strike me like the barroom brawl type."

"Excuse me. And I do?"

He grinned. "I suspect you're here about Denise McNaughton's murder, so let me update you. We're investigating, of course, following up several leads. Piecing together what might have happened. Coroner still hasn't given us an exact time."

"I've heard all those stock phrases before, Jim. You could offer a few facts. Lucas Prendergast has been sent to Utica for testing, I understand. Anything new on him?"

Fortunately, he couldn't resist a comment on that subject. "Actually, he's a pretty interesting guy. Why he chooses to live that way is a mystery to me. He's smart enough when you can get him to talk to you, but he doesn't know beans about what's going on in the real world. One thing that surprised me though—he seemed to know who you were right off, remembered you as a kid."

"I told you he was a friend of my grandfather's," I said.

Jim stared at me for a few seconds too long before he answered. "You realize that doesn't have anything to do with his guilt or innocence, don't you?"

"I know that," I assured him. Then I stood up fast and left

Somewhere along the line, I'd formed the habit when I drove away from the Municipal Center of rating my conversations with Jim. I scored this one a definite zero. In fact, if there'd been a lower grade I could have given it, I would have done so.

I needed to find an answer to at least one question before I went home to brood, and I had a thought. As long as I was still closer to Glens Falls than to Emerald Point, I could probably run down to the hospital and arrive there about the time Lee Townsend took her supper break. I'd come away from our conversation the other day with the feeling there was a lot she wasn't telling me. Maybe without the children to distract her, she'd be more forthcoming about Denise.

I pulled off the road and called her at work. Two tries and she came on the line. I told her straight out I wanted to ask her another question about Denise. She agreed I could meet her in the hospital cafeteria at six-thirty when she'd be taking her supper break. Perfect.

By the time I left the Northway at Exit 18, the sky over West Mountain had darkened to a deep rose gray, creating one of those perfect winter twilights. The five o'clock traffic had thinned to a manageable level as I drove along Broad Street, past the Hannaford shopping plaza and the recently refurbished Hudson Town Houses, now an attractive complex painted in soft pastels.

The hospital, situated not far from downtown, extended along Hudson Avenue, an imposing brick structure with the green glass highlights along the front entrance catching the last rays of the sun and its windows ablaze with light. Although it was surrounded by what appeared to be a sea of parking spaces, the lot was packed tight now with the cars of people making their evening visits to families and friends. Luckily, I knew to pull around back. I found a place there and made my way through a warren of corridors on the lower level until I located the cafeteria. I picked up a salad and coffee and positioned myself at a table where I would see Lee come in.

Ten minutes later, she hurried through the door, caught my eye and signaled she'd be right with me. After she'd picked up a cup of coffee, she joined me at the table.

"We're busy tonight. I'll have to make this fast." She shook out the contents of a brown paper lunch bag.

I waited while she'd fixed her coffee and unwrapped a tuna fish sandwich and a plastic bag of apple slices. Then I got right to the point. "Lee, I had the feeling the other day when we talked you started to tell me who Denise McLaughlin was seeing. Then you changed your mind."

She swallowed hard. "You're right, Loren. I decided I didn't want to spread the gossip. I suppose people here know, or at least suspect, but there hasn't been much talk. And it's better that way."

"You mean in case he's the guy who killed her?"

"Or in case he's the guy who didn't. Either way."

"So I guess it's somebody you know."

She hesitated, took a couple of bites of her sandwich.

Had I moved too fast? I was casting a net again, but I had no idea what I might catch.

"Well everybody here knows everyone else. This is sort of a closed society."

"I didn't think Denise stuck with guys she worked with. One name I've heard, the guy's not connected with the hospital at all."

Lee picked me up on that. "Are you talking about Tim Donohue? I heard she was seeing him. And you want to know the truth—I was pleased about that. He's not married, isn't involved with his ex-wife, doesn't have another girlfriend, as far as I know. So I'd say he was a step up for Denise. So of course, it didn't last."

"A step up?"

"Denise didn't make the best choices."

"You think she'd broken it off with Tim?"

"If she hadn't, I'd bet she was going to."

"And the other man? Someone connected with the hospital, I suppose?" I thought about what Billie had said about the doctors stopping in the recovery room to check on their surgical patients.

"I guess you could say that. We had something in common there. I tried to warn her."

"You tried to warn her?" I leaned forward. Was Lee about to tell me what I wanted to know?

"Yeah, but she wouldn't listen. And now she's dead." Lee shoved what was left of her sandwich aside and slipped the bag of apple slices into the pocket of her smock.

"You're not blaming yourself, are you? I've heard the gossip about the recovery room," I said.

"You're getting warm, Loren. You're getting very warm."

With that, she stopped herself. She pushed her chair back and stood up. "But I've got to get back. Sorry to rush off, but we're really busy tonight."

Before I could ask another question, before I could thank her for meeting me, she swung around and took off fast out of the cafeteria.

I did a lot of speculating on my ride home, but I didn't have enough information even for a guess. I was getting warmer, but not warm enough. Lee had come close to revealing something. She'd implied Denise might have been involved with one of the doctors, implied that she herself might have been at one time. But she hadn't said so. I couldn't jump to conclusions. It wasn't fair to anybody involved.

Still, the suggestion hung there, loud and clear.

Forty-five minutes later, when I walked through my kitchen door, I found the light on my answering machine throbbing as if in serious distress. I'd had five calls, it informed me, all of which were apparently urgent. I didn't stop to take off my coat. I pushed the play button.

"Loren, Teddie Murray, here," a familiar voice proclaimed. "Call me when you get in." The second message, left only a few minutes later, contained exactly the same words; the third repeated the command, but at a higher pitch with a sense of greater urgency. By the fourth and fifth messages, Teddie was frantic. "Loren, please. It's important. Call me the minute you get this."

I stifled a groan and punched in her number. This couldn't be anything short of a catastrophe

Teddie picked up on the first ring. Since she was close to hyperventilating, she didn't bother with hello. "Loren, did you see the crowds down near the Village? They're huge, absolutely huge. We've got to find a way to cash in on this Carnival thing."

"Cash in?"

Once I realized the world wasn't collapsing around us, I took a deep breath and used my free hand to rummage in the refrigerator for an open bottle of Chardonnay. I managed just enough self control to stop myself from taking a swig out of the bottle and reached into the cupboard for a wine glass. I poured a generous portion.

"We absolutely have to do something up here at Emerald Point," Teddie said.

I took a long, delicious sip. "What do you think it should be? So far, we haven't been able to agree on anything."

"We should have a couple of events of some kind, not just let the Village have them all. No reason we can't come up with something. It's short notice, but I think it's essential. Don't you?"

"Teddie, we talked about this before. We'd have to have something that doesn't compete with the Lake George Village activities."

I didn't have to explain. For several years the towns on the lake had honored an informal gentlemen's agreement that said when one community was offering a special event, the other towns would refrain from holding similar events at the same time. Non-compete was the term we used and the policy meant better relations between the towns.

"We don't have to have the same events," Teddie persisted. "We can think of something else. No reason we can't have a special activity too. It's school vacation week. We can bill it as something for the kids, but it will bring the parents and others here too."

"Let me touch base with a couple of people, see if I can get some support for this," I said. "In the meantime why don't you start makng a list of activities we could have that wouldn't conflict with the ones Lake George Village is planning."

As soon as I said the words, I had an idea—a brilliant idea, I thought at the time. It would be a perfect way of killing two birds with one stone. It didn't occur to me I could end up being one of those birds myself.

Chapter 15

Teddie Murray might rub me the wrong way at times but, as I thought about her suggestion, I had to admit the idea of a mini-carnival as an Emerald Point winter activity had definite appeal. All I needed was fifteen minutes of staring at the lake from the living room window to come up with a plan.

If we were going to schedule a winter event, we'd not only have to move fast to organize it, we'd have to create something totally different from the Lake George Village Winter Carnival. The Village had been holding their event for almost fifty years. During that time, they'd changed it, refined it, added new activities and done away with others, until in recent years it extended over the four February weekends and still managed to attract good sized crowds.

We'd have to plan ours for dates in February too, of course, when we could be sure the ice would be thick enough. If the cold temperatures continued the way they'd been the last two weeks, we'd be able to count on eight or ten inches of ice. And we'd have to offer totally different activities which wouldn't compete with those the Village featured every year.

Our first order of business would be to come up with something new. How hard would that be?

I grabbed a pen and a fresh tablet of paper and began a list. We could start with more modest activities, gear events toward a different age group, maybe the younger kids. Josie's words about taking advantage of what the area offered popped back into my mind. What if I invited her to be on the committee, pulled in a couple of other high school students and asked them to suggest activities which would appeal to a younger age group? That could create an entirely different atmosphere at the event.

Also—my mind went on racing—what about people like Jane

Kennison and Alice Simmons? Their idea of serving hot chocolate to the Plungers was a perfect example of thinking outside the box. Not only had they managed to add a different dimension to the event, their presence demonstrated that the Plunge attracted something other than a bunch of crazies. Here were some of the area's solid citizens finding a way to take part. And, yes, I admitted this thought occurred to me—if I could get Jane Kennison to participate in something happening in my world, I might get some fresh insights into her world as well.

Within two days I had my committee. I asked Teddie to chair a meeting the next Wednesday night at the Village Building. She was delighted, as I'd known she would be. I invited Jane and Alice who accepted at once, then added Pauline and her husband Reggie since I could count on them to bring their own brand of common sense. I also knew that between the two of them they would recall every winter carnival and cold weather event held at the lake for many years back, remember the crowd pleasers and steer us away from the activities which had fallen flat. I also included a couple of Village Board members for balance.

Was it Robert Burns who came up with that great line about the "best laid plans of mice and men?" He should have been at that first meeting we held at the Village Building.

I kicked things off and thanked everyone for coming. Then I introduced Teddie and turned the running of the meeting over to her.

As is sometimes the case with people who come on strong, Teddie, when faced with the chance she'd wanted to chair a meeting, fell apart.

She managed a few opening comments, which she'd apparently planned ahead, then pulled up short with no idea how to go on. She stammered out a couple of half-formed questions as she searched the faces of the others present, obviously hoping that someone would rescue her.

Jane and Alice glanced at each other, but neither spoke. After several awkward minutes, Josie Donohue got to her feet.

She pushed her hair back from her face and looked around the room. "I talked to some of the kids at school about what they'd like. One thing popular for little kids is a Rub a Dub Dub Tub. You can put two kids in a tub—you really just throw a cover over a big inner tube. You give 'em some bath toys and bubble stuff and somebody on skates pulls them around the ice. Not too fast, of course. A guy I know helped with it some place last year. He said the kids loved it."

Several nods and murmurs of approval from both the teens and adults present.

Josie continued with more confidence. "That could be a morning activity, maybe have other stuff in the afternoon. But the main thing—and a lot of the high school kids I talked to liked this idea—is to have figure skating. We'd need to rope off a rink, of course, and make it as smooth as possible. We can let anyone who wants to skate use it during the day. There could be special skating events, whatever the skaters would like to have, maybe even some kind of contests.

"Then in the evening we set up some lights and ask a couple of skating groups to put on a demonstration or something, and we could bring other skaters in on it too. Maybe we can get some professionals who teach figure skating classes to help us plan something."

Kirsten Ryan, one of Josie's friends who'd come with her, piped up, "You know what they've been saying—Lake George isn't just for summer anymore. That could be a kind of a slogan, our mantra really."

Jane leaned forward in her chair. "Excellent ideas, girls. And Josie, tell us more about the skating. Some of the docks on the cove have been pulled up for the winter, but others have been left in with ice eaters around them. We'd have to avoid any areas near them where the ice might be soft."

I held my breath, thinking Josie might be weak on the details. Those of us who lived on the lake understood the use of ice eaters to keep the water from freezing around docks. Ice could do tremendous damage along the shore, especially in the spring when it started to break up.

"We'd have to know exactly where the ice eaters and bubblers are before we plan the rink and keep the skating away from those places," she said.

"But you can see where there's open water, can't you?" Kirsten asked.

Josie was ready with her answer. "That's not good enough. The ice will be soft around the open water. Some people won't realize that. We'll have to be sure those places are marked off."

"Why couldn't we get people to turn off their bubblers for a day or two?" someone else said

Jane shook her head. "I'm not sure that's possible, or that a day or two would be long enough, but 1 can look into it for you. I'll talk to some people who use them."

"That would be great," Josie said. "Then we can figure out a place for the daytime activities and use the same area for the night skating."

Reggie, an old hand at meetings, cleared his throat. "You girls are cooking up some great ideas there. And there's a couple more activities you might want to think about besides the rink. Think about dog sled rides, especially good if you're considering the younger kids. Then maybe get George Taylor to bring his hot air balloon and inflate it. Even if nobody goes up in it, people love to see 'em, especially after dark."

By this time everyone was ready to talk and the suggestions came fast and furious. "A petting zoo if it's not too cold," somebody called out. "A chili cook-off," someone else added.

"And a bonfire," Josie's friend Emily said.

"On the ice? Won't it burn right through?" Bonnie Jo asked in surprise.

Emily giggled. "No. Of course we wouldn't have it on the ice. It would be on the shore. People could warm up by it. A bonfire on the shore at night would make everything perfect."

Josie got to her feet. "Emily had another idea some of us think would make a perfect evening activity—a Mardi Gras party."

"Mardi Gras?" somebody asked. "You mean like they have in New Orleans?"

"They have them in a lot of other places too, especially in Europe," Emily said. "Of course, ours wouldn't be that big a deal, but we could do some of the same things—people could wear costumes and masks. We could make decorations in purple, green and gold—those are Mardi Gras colors. Maybe we could even throw those beads around like they do in New Orleans."

"But isn't Mardi Gras celebrated just before Lent starts? Won't all the parades and parties in New Orleans be over before we do this?" someone said.

Apparently, Emily had done her homework on this subject too. "Mardi Gras means Shrove Tuesday. That's the day before Ash Wednesday when Lent starts. And yes, we'll be a little late. The actual date will have gone by, but not by much. And we couldn't have had our carnival on a week night anyway."

"And people would have to wear costumes and masks?" Pauline asked.

"It would be good if they did, but we wouldn't keep anybody out if they didn't want to dress up," Emily said.

Jane and Alice glanced over at me and smiled.

Once the group started talking, there was no stopping them. One of the girls—Marilee, I thought it was—pulled out a small pad of paper and started taking notes. "That might be a really good idea for the evening. Let's talk about it some more afterward. But what will we do in the afternoon?"

Pauline suggested two lists—one of activities we were considering and another of those we couldn't have without violating our agreement with Lake George Village. "That means no outhouse races," Reggie said with a grin.

Jane and Alice groaned, pretending to be disappointed. The outhouse races were loved or scorned according to individual sensibilities.

The room buzzed with suggestions until Jane got to her feet. "Look at the time," she said. "Let's plan on meeting again Wednesday. Is seven o'clock okay? And why don't we meet at my house? Emily, would you form a sub-committee and work up your ideas? Then Wednesday night, we can go outside and see where we'd put everything."

"Great idea," someone piped up.

And at the time I actually thought it might be.

Wednesday night when I arrived at Jane's house for the meeting, I found a group of our committee members gathered outside. I squeezed my car into a cleared spot off the circular drive which was already filled with cars and followed a shoveled walk down to the edge of the lake.

The house shimmered with light. Jane had turned on all the inside and outside lights as well as those around the dock. And as if they weren't enough, she and Alice were passing out an assortment of large flashlights and electric lanterns to the group.

She hurried over to me. "Loren, we're just about to go out on the ice and get an idea of where to put the activities we've talked about. We need to stay right in this area near the house. We don't want anyone to wander onto soft spots near the docks."

"Are there many docks here in the cove?" I asked. Although some of the docks had been winched up out of the lake; others had been left in the water for the winter.

"Most of the docks still in the water have ice eaters around them. We'll have to rope off sections, put up warning signs," Jane said.

"I thought we were going to get people to shut the ice eaters off for the carnival," one of the girls—I think it was Beth—said.

"Still wouldn't be safe," Jane told her. "The ice is soft for some distance around the ice eaters, and it might not freeze solid for quite a while after they're turned off."

With Alice's help, she rounded up the committee members, a high percentage of high school girls among them, and pointed out the areas to avoid. There were probably six or seven patches of open water, surrounded by the soft ice she'd talked about near the docks where the ice eaters were churning.

As she steered the group away from them, Jane went into even more detail to explain the problem. "This is very important. We'll rope off an area for our activities and we'll post warning signs over there by the docks. We'll have to be sure everyone stays away from those places. It shouldn't be too hard if we plan carefully. We've got a lot of open space on the lake with thick ice we can use for our events."

Josie and her friends forged ahead, armed with sketches of the activities they hoped to include. The temperature was dropping fast. Once on the ice, the girls were at the mercy of the wind and whatever they'd worn on their feet. Some of them with the right kind of boots, pranced along; others slipped and slid, grabbing onto one another to keep from falling.

"Look how smooth the ice is here." Josie, her scarf pulled up over her ears, paced off a section of the cove. "This area is perfect for the skating. It's almost like a rink now."

"Then we can put the little kids' games over here. There don't seem to be any bubblers anywhere near here," someone added.

Pauline picked her way over to me. "These kids are anxious to do a good job, if they don't freeze to death first. Hope we get a break with the weather."

"Have you heard any update for later in the week?" I asked her. Another storm had been forecast. I hoped it wouldn't come soon enough to shut down the whole project.

"Reggie will keep us posted, but it doesn't look too good," Pauline said.

Jane took the lead in delegating jobs and assigning girls to each event. Then, after each activity had been allotted a place on the ice, she called the group back together.

"Committee members should try to meet during the next few days, map out a plan for their area and prepare a list of what they'll need to bring to our next meeting. Now, let's all go warm up with some hot cocoa before that wind gets any more biting."

No one disagreed with that idea. The group moved en masse toward the house.

"Come this way. You're too close to the bubblers," Jane called out to two girls, who'd wandered away from the rest.

As the committee members spilled into the kitchen, Alice greeted us with a huge pot of cocoa and trays of sandwiches and cookies, always a welcome sight to teenagers. For people who didn't have children of their own, Jane and Alice seemed to know exactly how to create a successful experience for young people.

Half an hour later, the committee members, still bubbling over with talk, began filing out of the kitchen door, heading for their cars.

I was lingering behind to thank Jane and Alice for all they'd done, when Dr. Kennison squeezed through the kitchen door. "Are you people still at it? You must have something really special planned, if you've spent this much time on it."

Jane hurried over to him. "Sorry, Ed. I bet you couldn't even get into your own driveway, could you? I thought we'd be finished before you got home, but you're right. The committee had so many good ideas we just kept going."

"No problem," he assured her, "glad you're getting somewhere."

What was all this, I wondered. Here was the guy who was appearing all over town with another woman, and yet his relationship with his wife came across as perfect. Was this a stellar performance for our benefit, or was it possible that Jane didn't know what everyone else in town was buzzing about?

I added my good night and another thank you to Jane for her hospitality and followed the others out. Once in the driveway, I decided it might be safer to wait for the last of the young people to pull out before I crossed over to where my car was parked. After my trip with Josie a few days before, I wasn't anxious to take any chances with teenage drivers.

I lingered near the door, watching as cars backed out, jockeyed for a place in the circular drive and headed up the hill toward the highway. The north wind had gathered even more force and roared off the lake with a fury, setting the bare branches of the maples creaking and scraping against one another. I pulled my parka tight around me. Even the hot chocolate, now only a distant memory, didn't help ward off the cold.

"See ya, Lor," Josie called as she passed me in Kate's car and swung into the line of cars pulling out. She was doing okay, I realized. I could have watched her without holding my breath.

When most of the cars had passed me, I picked my way across the driveway and tugged my car door open. As I slid onto the seat, I tried to pull the door closed behind me, but it wouldn't move. It must be the wind, I thought first, but I turned back to see a dark form standing next to the car, a gloved hand gripping the edge of the door.

"Hey," I said.

"Loren, did I startle you?"

The Dr. Kennison leaning into my car had dropped the understanding husband act, and he didn't look anything like the cool guy in the expensive ski wear I'd seen at Gore. Even with his hat pulled low and his scarf obscuring the lower part of his face, I couldn't miss the scowl and the glint of hostility in his eyes.

"We meet again, Loren. I seem to be seeing a lot of you lately. At Gore, in the hospital cafeteria. Now here you are at my house. And a couple of weeks ago we scarcely knew one another."

His words, in themselves, were matter-of-fact, harmless even, but his tone, the inflection in his voice, the way he crowded into my space as he delivered them made me hear them as a threat. Startled, I pulled back.

"Jane offered to have the meeting here so we could check out the cove for the ice carnival." Probably one of the most inane remarks I'd ever made, but it was the best I could come up with.

"I see. That's the only reason you're here?" The tone was smug, disbelieving.

His presence had startled me; his manner made me uncomfortable, and now he was ticking me off. I was cold, tired and sick of meetings. A flock of teenagers, all talking at once, no matter how good their intentions, could drain anyone's vitality. I was giving up my evenings to plan an event which might prove a dismal failure or even be cancelled entirely if the storm hit us as predicted. And now this veiled threat.

"I came for a meeting, and I'm trying to leave," I snapped. I turned the key in the ignition and tugged on the door handle, trying to close it.

He jumped back. The sound of the engine had startled him, I was pleased to see, so I gave it a little more gas than necessary. He held onto the door a few seconds longer, then let go. I yanked the door shut hard. As I turned my lights on, he stepped back, as if he feared I might swing the car toward him, but I eased ahead carefully. The last thing I wanted to do was get stuck in his yard and have to rely on him for help. As soon as I hit the paved driveway, I accelerated and drove as fast as I dared up the hill.

On the way home, I replayed the exchange over and over. I was more shaken by his words that I wanted to admit. I'd sensed something threatening in his comments, but who would believe me? I couldn't imagine myself repeating them to Jim. Even Kate or Pauline would probably question my sanity. One of those "you had to be there" experiences we've all had.

And the bottom line, when I finally got around to admitting it to myself: I'd asked for it. I'd been hoping to uncover something about the doctor's web of secrets, and he'd seen through me. So had he threatened me? Was he warning me to bug off? It had sure felt like it to me.

Chapter 16

By the time I dragged myself out of bed the next morning after a restless night of interrupted sleep, I was ready and willing to admit my mistake. I'd been careless. I'd made my interest in Ed Kennison and his love life much too obvious. If I'd wanted answers to some of the questions surrounding Denise McNaughton's death, I should have taken a different approach.

Solving this kind of problem should be like peeling an onion—start at the edges and work your way in toward the center—that was always the best technique. I'd messed up by zeroing in too fast on the doctor himself.

About four o'clock, long before the first rays of light had penetrated my bedroom windows, an answer came to me. I knew the perfect person to chat with about the doctor and his relationships, and do it without being too obvious.

After two cups of coffee and a couple of pain killers which barely made a dent in the grandparent of all headaches, I drove to the office. An hour later, I called the radio station to ask if I could set up an appointment with Billie Jorgensen. Billie didn't come in until noon, the secretary told me, but I dropped the right hints. He called me back a little while later shortly after he got my message.

"I was thinking this would be a good time to do that interview on the Woodsman you suggested," I said.

"Been meaning to call you about that, Mayor. He was sent to a hospital in Utica, as I understand it, but I wouldn't be surprised if we're about ready to hear the next installment in that story."

"You can hold your report to whenever the time seems right, Billie. I also want to bring you some information about the winter carnival we're planning for Emerald Point. We can kill two birds with one stone," I said.

"You're not planning to compete with the Lake George Village Carnival, are you, Mayor? Thought that was a no go."

"No competition at all. We've got something totally different in mind and that's exactly why we need the publicity. Want people to understand that right from the start."

"Why don't you come down around two o'clock?" Billie said. "Give us some time to talk before I go on the air."

Perfect. That was exactly what I wanted.

I'd stopped in the radio station several times in the past when I wanted to make a pitch for one of our Emerald Point activities, but I always managed to forget how small and cramped it was.

The receptionist, huddled behind the counter near the front door, greeted me as if she'd been expecting me. She ushered me immediately into a cluttered space off the entrance which was crammed with electronic equipment I couldn't identify and two desks overflowing with papers and notebooks.

Billie came forward at once to greet me. "Sit here, Mayor," he said as he whipped a chair around, then sat down next to me by one of the desks. The man obviously didn't suffer from claustrophobia, or he would never have lasted in his job.

"Let's start with the Woodsman," he began. "You mentioned you have some background on him?"

"I knew him years ago when he used to visit my grandfather," I said.

"Great. First-hand report." Billie spent the next fifteen minutes asking who, what, where, why, when and how questions and listening carefully to my answers like the capable reporter he was.

I answered as accurately as I could, but didn't touch on my experience with the dropped oars. Instead, I called up a couple of other memories of the Woodsman from those lazy summer afternoons on my grandfather's porch.

"I get the feeling you don't see him as a murderer," Billie said.

"Definitely not. Also I've been told by a witness who doesn't want his name used that he was spotted up in the mountains that same day, too far away to have been anywhere near the murdered woman's house that night."

Billie's eyes opened wide. "How about a name here, Mayor? Anonymous sources don't carry much weight in a murder investigation, you know."

"That's the problem, Billie. You must have found yourself in this position more than once yourself. What do you do when you're told something in confidence and asked not to repeat it?"

He nodded. "Not a good situation to be in, I agree. But as I understand it, your problem's gone up in smoke anyway. From what I've heard tell, two days ago the Woodsman managed to high-tail it right out of that hospital in Utica and set out on his merry way. I suspect he's vanished back into the mountains by now."

I shook my head. I couldn't believe I was hearing right. "What are you saying, Billie? He's not in that hospital now? How do you know that?"

"I've got my sources, Mayor, same as you do. They haven't given the story out officially yet—a little embarrassing for the hospital and the sheriff's department both, you know—but he walked out of there two days ago and so far they haven't turned up any sign of him at all."

"You're sure of that?" I said.

"Sure as can be. Keep an ear open. I'll be talking about it on the air the minute they give me the go-ahead."

I saw Billie sneak a quick glance at the clock, so I produced the press release I'd put together on our winter carnival and handed it to him. "Not competing with Lake George Village, Billie. Some different activities for people up our way—I've listed them here. We're going to have all our events take place in the cove in front of the Kennison place. Jane's on the committee, and she's been great about helping us organize the carnival."

"The doc too? He helping out?" Billie gave me a knowing smirk.

"He's not on the committee, at least not right now. So I wouldn't want you to use his name in a broadcast," I said.

"Don't worry about that, Mayor. I peg him as one of those guys who manage to get themselves talked about, but then can't wait to jump down the throats of those who do the talking."

"There do seem to be rumors..." I left the sentence dangling, hoping Billie might add something.

"Ask somebody who works with him, if you want the facts. That's always the first place to start, I find."

But before I could decide how to phrase my next question, Billie lumbered to his feet and stuck out his hand for a good-bye handshake. Our conversation was over.

I walked out of the radio station berating myself for wasting my one chance to get information from Billie. I hadn't found any answers to the questions troubling me. As I pulled out of the station's parking lot and headed back toward Emerald Point, I replayed our conversation. Maybe, just maybe, I was jumping to conclusions too quickly.

When I thought back, I realized I hadn't asked much about the Woodsman, but Billie had offered information about him, and it had been a bombshell. He'd heard that Luke had walked out of the facility in Utica and disappeared. How could that be? The man could barely speak. He couldn't have had enough money to take public transportation. How could he possibly get himself out of there and back up into the mountains where he'd been living?

I'd assumed too that my efforts to learn something about Dr. Kennison had led nowhere as well. But had they? "Ask someone who works with him," Billie had said. I'd figured he was brushing me off, but maybe he'd told me exactly what I should do. Hadn't I already been going over my conversation with Lee, thinking she'd been deliberately holding back from telling me something. Talking with her at the hospital on her short supper break hadn't worked out very well. But if I could catch her at home…

Lee's house wasn't far out of my way. I could swing by and maybe, if I was lucky, catch her on a day off. Worth a try.

Luck was with me. Fifteen minutes later when I pulled up in front of her house, I spotted her car in the driveway. Looked like she was home, and mid-afternoon could mean nap time for the little ones and a chance to talk.

I didn't ring the bell. Even if I didn't have children of my own, I knew how important nap time could be to a harried mother. I tapped lightly on the door.

Lee opened it slowly and motioned me inside. "Come in, but let's not talk yet," she whispered.

She signaled me to follow her and led me down the hallway to the kitchen. Once she'd ushered me in, she shut the door behind us. "They're all asleep and that's not an easy trick to pull off nowadays. Want coffee? I was just having a cup."

"Lee, I'm sorry. This is probably not a good time to drop in on you."

"No. It's all right. They'll be awake before long. We might just have time for one cup before the onslaught." She pulled an old-fashioned percolator off the stove and poured me a cup, then topped off her own..

This wasn't the time to dawdle, so I didn't waste a minute. "Lee, I thought you started to tell me something more the last time we talked and then somehow we got sidetracked. You were going to say something about Ed Kennison."

"I guess maybe I was."

I waited.

She cleared her throat. "I saw him a few times outside of work."

"You mean you saw him out with someone?"

She curled her lip in disgust. "No. I mean I was the someone. I went out with him a few times myself before I came to my senses."

This wasn't what I expected to hear. When I totally blanked on the right response to that statement, I waited again.

"We had a couple of dinners in out-of-the-way places, very romantic, very hush-hush. After the second one, we went to a motel. I'd called in sick that night. My husband thought I was working. I don't know when I've ever felt so cheap."

"Then you didn't see him after that?"

"Oh no. I'm a slow learner. It took a couple more evenings like that before I told him I couldn't do it again"

"So you broke it off?"

"I like to think so, but the truth is he didn't protest too much. I think he was just as well pleased. Ed never lacked for chances. He moved on."

"Moved on?"

"You know about his affairs, don't you? Isn't that why you're asking me, to confirm what you already know? He moved on to Denise."

I took a quick mouthful of coffee. It was cold now. I didn't think I could get it down, but I managed it. I wished I had time to think. "Denise McNaughton?"

"That lasted quite a while. I think they were still together when she was killed. I was surprised it didn't come out then. But Denise didn't talk about her personal business, and of course, she lived up on that mountain where nobody was keeping tabs on her."

Nobody but Tim Donohue, I thought. He'd suspected Denise was seeing someone, and he'd tried to find out who it was. Had Ed Kennison been the other man in Denise's life, the man Tim had been talking about?

"But what about this girl he's being seen with now?" I asked.

I'd struck a nerve. Lee's leaned toward me, her face flushed with anger. "Being seen with? You mean making a spectacle of himself with, don't you?"

"He does seem to be pretty obvious about it."

"And she's not his usual type. Something's out of whack there. Plus, you're right about the way he's making sure everyone notices. That's not Ed's style at all."

"Lee, what are you saying?"

She stood up quickly and refilled her coffee cup. "Too much. I'm saying too much."

I needed confirmation, needed to be certain I'd heard her right. "I know he's being obvious with this girl, Lee. I saw them at Gore, myself. Other people have seen them skiing too, or out to dinner. He's not trying to hide her, that's for sure."

"No. He's putting his interest in her right out in the open. And you know, that disgusts me more than the other things he's done. He's using that girl, and she's too dumb to see it—or else she sees it, and wants to hang onto him so bad she's sitting back and letting him get away with it."

"But why the change this time?" I asked.

"You can't think of a reason?"

I saw where she was going with this, but I was reluctant to speak the words. "What am I missing here?"

"That he wants to be talked about, wants it bad enough to make a fool of his wife and humiliate that poor, stupid girl."

"And this is a departure from his usual style?"

"Loren, it's so obvious. You must see it. She's a red herring. He doesn't want it to come out that he was seeing Denise, especially now when he might be suspected of her murder."

Chapter 17

Sometimes when you're puzzling out something, you simply don't have enough information to come to an intelligent conclusion. At other times, your dilemma is just the opposite. You wrestle with information overload until your brain buzzes with all the possible ramifications. That's exactly what I was doing as I drove home.

What Lee had told me made perfect sense. If Ed Kennison had been seeing—that was apparently the way people liked to phrase it—Denise McNaughton at the time she was murdered, he'd naturally want to keep the news of their affair under wraps. And what better way to do it than an obvious romance with someone else? Unless, of course, the game Ed was playing was too blatant, and there was another reason for his behavior Lee didn't know about—or didn't want to.

I was still mulling over this conundrum when I pulled into my driveway and parked close to the house under the portico I'd had built the summer before for my car. The simple structure didn't have the advantages of a garage, but on nights like this anything that offered protection from the wind off the lake was a plus.

My headlights caught an unexpected shape near the house. A piece of trash? A branch blown down by the wind? I stared in astonishment. What I was seeing wasn't an inanimate object. Someone was huddled next to the steps. I reached into the back seat for the baseball bat I kept there and opened the car door slowly.

As I approached the house, the dark form stirred and moved its limbs in an awkward, disjointed way. I lifted the bat, ready to swing if I had to.

"Missy, can you help me?" A man's voice—low, scarcely more than a croak. Then a long pause as he struggled to find words for what he wanted. "I've got to find John Graham. Rang bell, doesn't answer."

"John Graham? You're looking for John Graham?"

"Yes. This his house?"

I didn't know how to answer his question. Yes, it was true my grandfather, John Graham, had lived his entire life in this house, but he'd been dead for over seven years.

I loosened my grip on the bat. I realized now who my unexpected visitor was. I didn't want to frighten him. I forced myself to speak in a calm, even tone. "Luke? Luke Prendergast? Is that you?"

"Is John home? Need to warm up. John would let me come in, warm up."

"John's not here, Luke. I'm Lorie. I live here now."

He studied my face. "Lorie?"

"His granddaughter."

"... all grown up now."

"Yes. Remember I came to see you last week at the jail."

"Lorie. You came to see me. Can I come in, get warm?"

What choice did I have? At that moment, I asked myself the same questions I'd be asking Jim Thompson the next time I saw him, as he was slapping me in irons and hauling me off to jail. What else could I have done?

I didn't hesitate. I unlocked the back door. "Come in, Luke."

Luke followed me into the kitchen, his movements slow and unsteady. He pulled off a matted wool cap. I didn't suggest he sit down at the table, but showed him into the downstairs bathroom and handed him a washcloth and towel. He was wearing what appeared to be his own clothes, not something from a jail or hospital—a threadbare jacket and jeans caked with soil. I closed the door behind him and went back to the kitchen to rummage through the cupboard and refrigerator.

I thought about what I was doing. Billie Jorgensen said Luke had escaped from the Utica hospital, and Billie usually got the facts first-hand. Usually, but not always. Maybe Luke had been released and was headed back into the mountains. I was offering him temporary respite on his journey. Worst case—he'd escaped and half the law enforcement agencies in the North County were tracking him and would descend on me any minute. I didn't want to go there. But in either case, the bottom line remained the same—this guy was cold and hungry, and he needed my help.

I didn't have a lot of choices for an impromptu meal. I settled on tomato soup, emptied a can of it into a bowl, added milk and popped it into the microwave. While it heated, I piled cold meat and cheese into the biggest sandwich I could concoct. Then, as I thought about how cold he must have felt as he huddled outside, I pulled out a frying pan and grilled the sandwich so at least he'd be getting something warm. Fortunately, I had enough milk to give him a glass along with the tail end of a package of cookies.

As I was setting the food on the kitchen table, Luke came limping across the kitchen and dropped into a chair.

"....smells good," he said.

"You must be hungry, Luke."

He didn't reply, but almost before I'd finished saying the words, he'd devoured most of the soup and half the sandwich.

Ten minutes later, Luke had polished off everything I could find, including an assortment of leftovers I retrieved from the refrigerator. He wasn't a guy who talked while he ate other than uttering a couple of thank you's. As soon as he'd finished every crumb, he shoved himself away from the table and, without saying anything more, headed back toward the bathroom.

I slid the dishes into the dishwasher and paced around trying to decide what to do about him. It was after ten o'clock, late to call Jim Thompson, although somebody would be on duty at the sheriff's office, ready and willing to answer the phone. And then what? Would they send a car after Luke and take him back to jail?

I'd washed off the counter and table and made myself a cup of decaf before I realized Luke had been gone a little too long. I hurried to check. Although I hadn't heard him come out of the bathroom, the door stood open. The room was empty. A few steps more, and I saw Luke lying face down on the couch in the living room, his breathing slow and heavy. He was sound asleep.

"Luke, wake up." I called his name half a dozen times, even shook his arm. He didn't stir.

I went back to the kitchen, sat down again at the table and finished my coffee. I stalled a few minutes longer, then made another attempt to wake Luke. No sign he was going to come to. I didn't know how he'd managed to get from the hospital in Utica to Emerald Point, but it wasn't hard to tell he was exhausted.

I covered him with the afghan off the back of the couch and left enough low light that he could find his way to the bathroom if he woke up. Although I acknowledged to myself I wasn't totally comfortable with Luke in the house, I went upstairs. At that point I couldn't think of any other way to deal with this problem. Even if I did manage to wake him up, I certainly wasn't going to send him back out in the bitter cold. The only other alternative was to call the sheriff's department and have him carted off to jail. A night on my couch seemed like the best alternative.

I didn't undress, just kicked off my shoes and slid into bed. I must have dozed off, or come very close to it, when the clatter of footsteps on the stairs startled me awake. I bolted up in bed, my heart racing. Was that Luke pounding up the stairs? Was that his voice shouting my name? How could I have been so sure he wasn't violent, that he wouldn't come up here and try to murder me?

The bedroom door crashed against the wall. Don Morrison, visible only as a dark form in the light from the hall, banged into the room. "Loren, wake up for God's sake. Who the hell is that guy on your couch?"

My heart beat slowed. I was relieved; I had to admit it. "Don, is that you? I didn't think you were coming back tonight."

I felt him reach across me and switch on the lamp on my night stand. I squinted, and threw my arm over my eyes.

He stared down at me, his face contorted with anger.

"Weren't you supposed to stay in Albany? Isn't that what you said?" Even as I asked the questions, I realized how stupid they sounded under the circumstances.

"Loren, who is that sleeping on your couch in the living room? I hope to hell it's not who I think it is."

I was never at my best when I first woke up, especially after less than a half hour of sleep, and this would have been a tough question to answer if I'd been in tiptop form. I countered with a question of my own. "Who do you think it is? Did you think I'd brought a new guy into my life?"

"Damn it, Loren. This is no joke. It's that Woodsman, isn't it? How the hell did he get out of jail? Don't tell me you went and bailed him out?" Don's voice rose to an irritating pitch as he hurled one question after another at me.

It was late; I was tired; and I didn't have good answers to give him. I felt my own anger building to a dangerous level. "Keep your voice down. No sense waking him up," I hissed.

"Keep my voice down?" he bellowed. "Why? So I won't disturb some vagrant, some acknowledged crazy who might have come up here and killed you?"

I took a deep breath and fought for what was left of my self-control. I struggled to speak in a reasonable tone. "He came here because he thought my grandfather would take him in."

"Your grandfather? He's that far out of it he thought your grandfather was still alive?"

"Don, he was huddled near the back door when I came home. He was cold and desperate—and really hungry. I made him something to eat, and the next thing I knew, he'd fallen asleep on the couch."

"Wait. You've not only taken him in and let him sleep here, you fed him too?"

As if I shouldn't have done any of those things. "All corporal works of mercy, if I recall my Sunday school lessons correctly," I said.

"Damn it, Loren, you know nothing about this guy. He's lived like a wild man up in the mountains for a good part of his life. He could have killed you."

I had to acknowledge what he said was true. I felt my last shreds of patience slipping away. "All right. We'll wake him up. You can see for yourself what he's like. Maybe if you'd talk to him, you'd get a better idea of how we can help him."

That idea set him off again. "Help him? Loren, listen to what you're saying. It's not your job to help him. He needs to be in a medical facility, some place where he can get professional help."

I threw back the covers and scrambled out of bed. "Damn it, that's enough. Don't say anything more. I'll try to wake him and you can talk with him or not, but I don't want any more advice about him."

Don stared at my sweater and slacks. "You went to bed fully dressed? You must have been worried enough about what he might do that you went to bed in your clothes. Do you think clothes would stop him if he decided to come up here and murder you?"

I didn't answer. I shoved my feet into my shoes and slipped past him out of the bedroom. Before he could react, I was on halfway down the stairs. I heard him hurrying after me, but I didn't slow down.

The minute I reached the living room, I knew what had happened. I could see the couch in the light coming from the kitchen. It was empty. Luke was gone.

Chapter 18

"Damn it, Don. He must have heard us. He's gone."

I made a quick check of the other rooms, but I didn't expect to find Luke in any of them. The afghan from the couch was gone. I hoped he'd taken it. It wouldn't do much to protect him from the cold, but it was something. I grabbed my parka and hat off the hook near the back door and threw them over a chair while I rummaged around on the closet floor for my warmest pair of boots.

Don stood watching me. "Loren, what are you going to do?"

"What do you think I'm going to do? I'm going to try to find him before he freezes to death out there." I shoved my arms into my coat.

"Don't you think you should call the sheriff's department?"

"No. I don't think that. If I'd been going to do that, I would have called them when I first saw him. Where the hell are my heavy gloves?" I pawed through the pile of hats and gloves on the shelf above the coats.

"Loren, calm down. I'll help you find him. I'll go with you."

"Forget it, Don. I don't want your help." I pulled the gloves off the shelf along with a wool scarf I could wrap around my head and neck. I could hear the wind roaring off the lake, even stronger than it had been an hour earlier.

"Loren, he can't have got far in that amount of time. We'll find him."

"I'll find him. You go home. You've done enough damage for one night."

Even as I said the words, I realized I'd crossed a line, but I was too angry to care. I didn't look at him. I grabbed my car keys and slammed the door as I went out.

Luckily, Don had parked far enough away from my car that I could ease around him. I inched out of the yard and up the hill, my eyes searching every shadow, every pull-off and driveway. No sign of Luke. No fresh footprints in the snow. When I turned north on the main road, I saw tire tracks near the edge of the pavement as if a car had pulled off, but that didn't mean that Luke had flagged down a ride there or that someone had picked him up.

I pressed on, trying to reassure myself. Would anyone refuse a hitchhiker on a night like this? There was no way I could know what might have happened to Luke. I assumed he was headed north, back into the mountains, but even that, I couldn't know for sure.

I crept along at a snail's pace, pulling off on the shoulder whenever there was adequate space to stop. I took time to turn into some of the driveways that led to farmhouses or barns, searching for fresh tracks or signs that someone had walked on the road recently.

I couldn't have said how much time I'd spent or how many false leads I followed before I finally gave up and drove home. Don's car was gone from the driveway. I was relieved. I couldn't handle another argument.

I left both the outside pole lamp and the kitchen light on, and I didn't lock the back door in case Luke turned up again and wanted to come in. I knew there was little chance of that happening, but somehow it made me feel better to think the house was open to him if he did come back. I blocked all thoughts of Don. When I fell into bed, I didn't think I could sleep, even though it was after three o'clock, but in only a few minutes I felt myself drifting off.

The next morning when my eyes popped open a little before seven, I wanted nothing more than to burrow under the covers and fall back to sleep, but I couldn't do it. The ice carnival was scheduled to start that afternoon, I didn't have time to worry about Luke, but I kept thinking about him. I drove to the office and typed a couple of letters I needed to send out. Then, with the most essential work done, I called Pauline to see if she could come in an hour early.

When she arrived, I let her start on her next project, typing up the minutes of the last Board meeting, before I asked the question tossing around in the back of my mind. "Ever hear of a guy named Brad Thomas, Pauline?"

"You mean the one who tends bar at Red's Tavern? Thirty-five or forty. If I'm not mistaken, he's one of the Thomases from the Warrensburgh branch of the family. Why do you ask?" She narrowed her eyes, a sure sign Pauline's early warning system was kicking in.

I couldn't believe it had been this easy. "Nothing important. Somebody mentioned him lately. Wondered what kind of a guy he was."

"Hunter. Likes to get out in the woods. Never had much in the way of jobs. Don't know one way or the other about his character. Must be some reason you're wondering about him all of a sudden."

"Just curious, Pauline. Heard his name lately, that's all."

My answer seemed to satisfy her, although with Pauline I never could be sure. She went back to her typing.

Red's Tavern wasn't more than a fifteen minute drive away. Tucked in a dilapidated brick building on the western edge of Emerald Point, Red's didn't have much to recommend it, but I figured I could drop in around noon time without arousing too much suspicion.

"Brad Thomas working today?" I asked the bartender lounging behind the bar.

"Brad, somebody looking for you out here," he yelled.

The half-dozen guys seated on bar stools, swung around as one to look me over.

"Mayor Graham? What the hell are you doing in here?" one of them said. So much for not arousing suspicion.

I nodded a greeting. I was still trying to think of an answer when a man poked his head out of the door behind the bar, then sauntered out. He was dark-haired and lanky with a big food-stained apron tied over his jeans and a flannel shirt.

"Brad?" I said. "Can I talk to you a minute?" I stepped back away from the bar and lucked out when he followed me to the side of the room where I didn't think we could be overheard.

I took a deep breath, not at all sure how this was going to go. "I want to ask you something about Luke Prendergast—you know who I mean, the guy they call the Woodsman? Heard you might have seen him up in the mountains the same day Denise McNaughton was murdered."

"That Doug come and talk to you, did he? He gave me a heads up he might be gonna do that."

"He talked to me, and I tried to get him to go to the sheriff's investigator about it. Would mean a lot to that poor guy if somebody would speak for him." Then I waited. I didn't think it could possibly be this easy, but maybe, just maybe...

And of course, it wasn't.

"No way, Missus. Doug said he made sure you understood he wouldn't be talkin' to the sheriff. And I'm a lot more hard-hearted than he is. No way am I gonna get involved in some murder case."

"But..." I started, although I wasn't at all sure what I could say that might change his mind.

"But, nothing. No way. Forget it. And don't be giving my name to the sheriff either. I'll deny I ever saw the guy—or you either. I'll tell him you made the whole thing up." He turned away fast and headed back to the kitchen.

Of course, I should have known. For a minute there, I'd hoped I could convince him. This was a dead end. Time to admit it.

I didn't linger in the bar, and nobody seemed sorry to see me go. I beat it out fast and headed to the cove to check out the preparations for our big event.

Since this was our first attempt at a winter carnival, the committee had decided to start with a sampling of activities on Friday afternoon and evening, work out any glitches and count on Saturday to be the big day. A sensible approach, it had seemed at first, but now a development we couldn't control—the weather forecast was predicting snow. ETA—sometime late in the day Saturday. Definitely not good news in this part of the world—the report of a nor'easter moving our way along the Atlantic coast. Looked like trouble ahead, unless we lucked out.

Shortly before three o'clock, I knocked on Jane's back door.

Jane, with Alice close behind her, swung it open. They were both already dressed in heavy parkas and boots. "We're just coming out, Loren. We've invited some friends to help. We expect the young people will be piling in here the minute they get out of school."

Jane was right, A few minutes later, cars overflowing with high school kids were crowding into any available parking places along the cove. Josie and her friends unloaded ropes, ice picks and assorted pieces of equipment and began to cordon off the area designated for the skating rink. While they busied themselves with that, Millie, the group's acknowledged artist, set an easel on the shore and nailed up a brightly painted sign with the words, Lake George Isn't Just For Summer Anymore, printed on it in huge letters.

Josie yelled over to me. "Do you like the sign, Lor? Millie's good, isn't she? Where do you think we should have the sleigh rides for the little kids? We may not get many tonight, but it will give us a good chance to test everything out."

"You decide. You seem to be on top of things," I called back.

Jane smiled. "You're right. These kids seem to be doing a terrific job."

"Good to hear," I said, and I meant it.

I stood with Jane and Alice, watching as a group of the young people roped off the rink area. To our left on the shore, several girls debated among themselves about where the refreshment stand should go.

The three of us exchanged smiles, but we all resisted the temptation to offer suggestions. The hardest part of working with new volunteers of any age was letting them make decisions and learn for themselves what worked and what didn't.

Once everyone was occupied, Jane turned to me, "Loren, as long as you're here, this might be a good time to tell you our plans for the property. Perhaps you've already heard the rumors. We'd like to build a new place. This one has become impossible to keep up, and we own enough land here to build something else."

"A new place? Where?" I'd heard the rumors like everyone else in town, but I'd held off believing them. The local gossip mill wasn't always accurate.

"We own most of this lakefront here on the cove. We want to build over there to our left, about where those girls are standing." She waved toward the spot where the committee was marking off space for the refreshment stand.

"And do what with this house?" I turned and glanced back. The Kennison house, which most people in Emerald Point considered one of the most attractive on the lake, stood three stories high with white clapboards, black shutters and a roof I'd exchange mine for in a minute.

"It has so much wrong with it, Loren. We're not sure there's much point in trying to save it. We're thinking we'd be better off to start over and build something new."

I couldn't hide my astonishment, and I didn't try. "You're not talking about a tear-down, are you?"

"Oh no. Not unless it comes as the last resort. I think we could have the house moved. Someone would probably take it off our hands and fix it up."

"Fix it up? Jane, it's a beautiful house."

Jane raised her eyebrows as if I were a child who'd just said something incredibly stupid. "Oh, Loren. It needs so much in the way of repairs—heating, roof, I can't begin to tell you all that's wrong. I'll have to give you a tour some time. These places on the lake take a real beating from the elements, you know."

Of course, I knew. I lived in one. My grandparents' place got hit hard by storms off the lake too, but that didn't mean I wanted to tear it down or give it away. I glanced at Alice, hoping to gage her reaction, but she had walked off.

"You're thinking of building something else here. Bigger and better, I suppose? Some kind of McMansion?" I couldn't suppress the note of disdain in my voice.

She smiled, but she jammed her hands into her pockets. "I'll call you the next time we have a storm and the roof leaks and the cellar floor gets soaked through. You'll see."

She turned and walked back toward the house. My comment had offended her. She'd made that obvious.

The activities we'd planned for that day went off almost as scheduled. If I'd been asked to rate our initials efforts at a winter carnival, I couldn't have given them more than a C at the most. The skating went well at first—probably 20 or 30 people turned up to take part—but by eight o'clock the wind had driven all but the hardiest skaters rushing for cover.

Even the hot dog vendor, who'd been doing a great business, packed up after an hour or so, wheeled his cart back up the hill to his van and took off. The man who'd agreed to bring his hot air balloon and keep it inflated near the edge of the cove called to say it wasn't a good night for it. He blamed the wind.

When Kate arrived unexpectedly after a party she'd catered, I wasn't shy about accepting a cup of soup from a big thermos she'd brought with her. Kate's cream of chicken soup with vegetables provided a life-saving infusion of warmth and nourishment. She waved aside my efforts to pay her. "I'm not charging. Consider it my contribution—and before you say no, think about the bad press you'll get when people start freezing to death out here."

"I wouldn't have the strength to refuse whether I wanted to or not. You're saving the day," I told her as others flocked around to sample the soup. "I don't think anyone could hang around much longer without something to warm up with."

Unfortunately, I was right. The few skaters left began drifting away. Within an hour we were down to only the committee members.

Shortly after nine, Jane called me over to where she was standing. "Loren, I went into the house a few minutes ago and called our Beach Club. George is willing to stay open a little while longer. He'll have pizza ready for the committee, and we can evaluate how tonight went and plan for tomorrow. I think these kids deserve a reward of some kind for all their hard work, and if the storm hits as predicted, we won't be able to get together tomorrow night."

I nodded, speechless with surprise. Invitations to the Beach Club were not easy to come by. This was the summer place for the wealthier families at the Point. The Beach Club nestled into the shore a few miles south of here, a simple, wood-framed building on the outside, but elegantly decorated and furnished within. Few outsiders were included in the parties and dances. Even Kate, despite her growing reputation, seldom got a catering gig there. The chef and his well-trained staff handled most of the parties and weddings. I'd been invited to a meeting there once or twice, but only because I was mayor. By no means could I think of myself as a regular.

Jane and Alice passed the word to Josie and the rest of the committee. Nothing like the promise of a party to get workers moving faster. In less than twenty minutes, the picking up was done. As the young people headed for their cars, Jane stopped each group to explain how to find the secluded driveway which led to the Club.

"This is a great thing for you to do," I told her. "You're probably responsible for the fastest clean-up in recorded history. They're so excited by the idea of this party."

"I'll try not to keep them too long. I've told John to serve something he and his staff can prepare quickly, and I'm sure he'll do it. He's always accommodating."

"You've arranged it already?" I asked.

."I told him the committee might want to get together at the Club tonight, and John's setting things up. I expect he'll serve mostly pizza, but that usually goes over big with this age group, don't you think? No alcohol for the kids, of course, but we adults can have a drink in the bar if we like."

"Sounds good." I knew a party at the Beach Club would be a perfect reward for the committee's hard work and help make up for the disappointment about the weather. I glanced over at Josie. She was beaming from ear to ear.

Most of the crowd had taken off fast, anxious to get to the Club. I made one final check of the cove and trudged up the hill to my car, relieved to see no sign of the doctor on my way.

I drove south along the highway until I spotted the marker Jane had described. It was small and so discreet I almost missed it. I turned left onto a narrow road which led down toward the lake. The Club wasn't easy to find, but it didn't have to be. The members knew the way, and drop-ins weren't encouraged.

By the time I reached the small white frame building, the parking area was jammed. I found an empty space at the far end and hurried back toward the entrance.

As I crunched along in the parking lot, a dark figure lurched out of the shrubbery. "Miss Lorie." Lucas Prendergast, looking even colder and scruffier than he had when I'd found him outside my door the night before, limped toward me. He wore the same clothes, that same inadequate jacket and pants he'd probably been wearing for who knows how long. The soiled cap was pulled low over his ears.

"Luke, what are you doing here? I spent hours searching for you last night. I thought you must have gotten a ride and gone back to ..." I forced myself to stop talking I had no idea where he might have gone back to. As far as I knew, he didn't have a home, even so much as a cabin, nothing but that lean-to the search party had found. Where would he have gone?

He came closer. "Looking for you," he said.

"Looking for me? Good. Come with me now. Let's go back to my house. You can get warm, and I'll make you something to eat?"

"No. No. Must tell you."

"Tell me?"

"Those people, Lorie. Not good, shouldn't be with them."

"Luke, what people? I don't know what you mean."

"There. Look there." He grabbed my arm and pulled me off the walk and through the snowy yard toward a window. He pointed inside.

The interior of the club gleamed with light. Crystal chandeliers glistened, spreading golden circles on the floor.. The sconces on the walls cast a warm rose glow. Soft contemporary music played on the stereo, underscoring the voices of the young people gathered around a long table loaded with trays of pizza.

I could hear snatches of conversation, laughter, friendly disagreements about which pizza was the best. "They're happy, Luke. They're having fun."

As I said the words, it occurred to me that Luke had probably never been to a party like this, never shared this kind of carefree time with friends. What had his life been like in the mountains, living hand to mouth, surviving on next to nothing?

"No. No. Not them. There. There." He pointed past the part of the room where Josie and her friends were gathered toward a small anteroom, almost hidden behind a wall. Jane and Alice and several of the other women who'd helped with the ice carnival clustered together in a tight group in front of a bar. A man in a white dress shirt and black bow tie behind it, served drinks.

As I watched the scene, Dr. Kennison stepped into my line of vision and next to his wife.

Luke grew more agitated. He shuffled through the snow, struggling to get closer to the window. He turned back to me and tried to speak, then stopped as if unable to find the words he wanted. He pointed at the doctor. "There. There. See those people. They're bad, Lorie."

"That's Dr. Kennison, Luke. Do you know him?"

"Bad. He's bad, Lorie. Don't go in."

He jabbed his finger at the window. Ed Kennison glanced in our direction, then frowned and moved nearer, peering out.

I grabbed Luke's arm and drew him back away from the building. "Luke, I have to go in for a minute. They're expecting me. Why don't you wait in my car? Then we'll go to my house and get something to eat. I know you must be worn out and ready for a hot meal."

To my surprise, he let me guide him back through the parking lot. I opened my car door and helped him into the passenger seat. I would have liked to turn on the engine and the heater, but I didn't quite dare. I didn't know if I could trust him not to try to drive off before I got back.

"Stay here, Luke. I'll be back in ten minutes. All right? You can wait here for a few minutes, can't you? Then we'll go and get something to eat."

When he appeared docile and settled back in the front seat, I shut the door. "Ten minutes," I said again. "I'll come back and we'll go get something to eat."

I hurried back across the parking area and up the walk to the front door.

Warm air hit me as I walked in. Warm air and the tantalizing aroma of pizza, and the sound of music, a lively beat underscoring the voices of the teenagers.

Josie, huddling with a group of her friends, called to me. "Lor, isn't this the best party? Everybody's getting a kick out of being here."

Jane waved from the bar. "Loren, join us. Come and have a glass of wine, and George will let you sample whatever pizzas you want to try. You can see for yourself why everyone loves them."

As I approached her, Dr. Kennison turned his back and began an earnest conversation with the bartender. Was he avoiding me? I suspected he was, but I couldn't be sure.

"I really should get home, Jane. The kids seem to be having a great time. This is a terrific thing for you to do."

"Not to worry. George is making sure none of them gets alcohol and the minute they finish their pizza, he's shooing them out the door. You can count on him."

I thanked Jane again and left. How much time had I taken? Five minutes? Ten, maybe? I hadn't lingered. I'd said what I needed to say and left immediately.

But I was too late. Luke wasn't in my car, and there was no sign of him in the parking lot. He'd taken off.

Chapter 19

Maybe if I hadn't spent so much time looking for Luke the night before, maybe if I'd had the patience for one more frustrating search, I would have driven around again and tried to find him. But there was no point, I told myself. He'd elude me tonight just as he had before. I went back into the Club.

The group at the bar welcomed me back. Even Ed Kennison was all smiles.

Jane came forward and took my arm. "Loren, I'm so glad you decided to stay. What would you like? Wine? A mixed drink?"

I ordered a Chardonnay and listened to the comments from the committee members. "We're off to a good start," Alice said, "and the kids are coming up with some new ideas for tomorrow. The wind slowed things down a little today, but this is shaping up to be an excellent first effort."

"And it will be a lot easier to do again next year, now that we've laid the groundwork," Jane added.

Ed Kennison swung around and held up his glass. "I think we should all drink to Loren. She's done a fabulous job helping us kick off our first winter carnival. And the way she got these young people involved has made all the difference. They've been a terrific help."

"Hear. Hear." Several of the other committee members at the bar joined in and raised their glasses too.

I didn't comment. I concentrated on smiling and sipping my wine. Dr. Kennison apparently had different personalities for different occasions. This was not the same guy who'd snarled at me in his driveway the night before. I glanced over at Jane. I couldn't read her expression.

A few minutes later, the bartender whispered to Jane and then disappeared into the dining room. "Sorry, guys," I heard him say to the group still gathered around the pizza. "We're about ready to close up. We'll pack up the rest of the pizza for anyone who wants it."

A waiter produced doggie bags for those who asked for them, and in no time the young people were headed for their cars.

Jane reached for her coat. "Time for us to go too, I guess. Let's plan on getting together in the morning, Loren, maybe around ten o'clock."

I thanked her again and took off. Even in this short time, most of the cars had pulled out of the parking area, their tail lights forming a trail of red up the hill. As I walked to my car, I looked for any sign of Luke. Nothing. He'd managed to disappear again.

On the drive home I considered what I would say to Don. It was Friday night. When he was working in Albany, he usually came back for the weekend, although whether he would come to my house after our argument or spend the night at his own place, I couldn't begin to guess.

I didn't have to.

I pulled into the yard slowly, thinking I might find Luke huddled by the door again, but there was no sign of him. The house was dark. Don wasn't there either and, if I was assessing the situation correctly, he wasn't going to be. In his mind, I was in the wrong again.

It took another large glass of wine and two cups of cocoa before I fell into an uneasy sleep.

When I arrived at the cove the next morning, I found Josie and a group of her friends gathered near their cars in the parking area, heads together in earnest conversation. She motioned to me to join them.

"Lor, what do you think of this idea? We'll make tonight's skate our version of Mardi Gras, like we talked about, but we won't call it that since the real Mardi Gras in New Orleans has gone by this year. We'll call it Carnival."

Wasn't it too late for that big a change? I bit my tongue. "Tell me what you have in mind."

"It could be fun, Lor—costumes, beads, masks. You said we should have something different than the activities they have down at the Village. This would be really different."

"Can people get costumes together on such short notice?"

"Sure. A lot of people have them anyway from Halloween parties. And Billie Jorgensen said he'd announce it on his radio program and get the other newscasters to do it too. We can let people know that way. And we'll all spread the word."

"But what about the people who don't hear?"

"Nobody has to dress up. Some people don't like doing stuff like that anyway. It's just a chance to do it if they want to."

"Have you talked this over with Mrs. Kennison? What does she think?"

"You can ask her yourself." Josie pointed to Jane who was walking toward us.

"I'm all for it," Jane said. "We went to New Orleans to Mardi Gras the year before Katrina, and we had a spectacular time."

I hadn't planned on a costume, but I could probably think of something. "If everyone agrees, why not?"

The day's activities started that morning and, despite a cold North wind, progressed more smoothly than I would have believed possible. Pete, the hot dog man, returned with his stand and did a steady business. The committee organized skating races for the younger kids, followed by another wild broomball game, fortunately with no major casualties.

In the late afternoon I took a short break and drove home to find a costume. I rummaged through a couple of closets, finally decided on my grandfather's bright yellow rain gear, not the most fashionable of outfits, but it would allow me to be warmly dressed underneath. I wasn't going to admit it to anybody, but I'd tugged on my new nylon-fiber long johns and long-sleeved shirt under my clothes. No one need know, I told myself, and they'd offer at least some protection from the freezing stabs of wind.

When I got back to the cove, the first group in costumes had gathered at the benches along the shore to put on their skates. The forecast had hit it right. The snow was holding off, at least for a time, and the committee had everything ready for the evening skating.

Billie Jorgensen, along with a couple of assistants, trucked his equipment down the hill and set up for a live broadcast. A boy band, known as the Mountain Lions from one of the area high schools, staked out a place nearby and tuned up, ready to provide music for the skating.

I eased my way down the bank and found a place to put on my skates. I stumbled as I took my first tentative glides on the ice. I'd skated as a kid, of course, and I'd been practicing a little this winter, but the old skills weren't coming back the way I'd hoped they would. I was definitely out of my league here, no match for the other skaters already zooming past me.

Josie skated toward me at top speed and careened up to me with a flourish. She wore what looked like an antique wedding gown, all white, with a floral headpiece and about a dozen strings of multi-colored beads hanging around her neck.

"You look great," I said, "but tell me you've got something warm on underneath that. If you don't, you're going to freeze to death."

"Sure. I'm all set, but you've got to get more into the spirit here, Lor. You don't look festive enough."

"I'm festive," I assured her.

"Wait. I've got an idea." Josie lifted about half her strings of beads and pulled them off over her head. She skated closer to me, dug a toe into the ice and reached up to drop five or six necklaces over my head.

"Wait. Why are you giving me your beads?" I asked her.

"Lor, they're genuine Mardi Gras beads. They bring good luck, and you'll need it if this storm hits us the way they're talking about."

"But, they go with your outfit."

"I gotta take some off anyway. They're getting in my way. I could have done without this many."

"Okay. Thanks. I'd be crazy to turn down a chance at good luck."

What did I know? Beads that brought good luck, even worn over a yellow slicker, might be just what we needed to delay the arrival of the storm.

Josie grabbed my arm and turned me around. "Lor, look. Here's Tommy. Doesn't he make a perfect vampire?"

Tommy Davidson, dressed all in black, skated over to us and grabbed Josie around the waist. After I'd agreed that he made a terrific vampire, Josie insisted he open his mouth to show ugly-looking fake incisors, made even more repulsive with the addition of red paint.

"Blood—the perfect finishing touch," I agreed.

His wasn't an original choice, however. As the young people flocked onto the ice, I counted more than a dozen vampires. A sign of the times with the popularity of True Blood and the other vampire stories. I should have known. I particularly liked one gruesome couple—the guy, a vampire with the handle of a knife protruding from his chest, and the girl with him dressed in a dance costume of some kind with a parka underneath and a blood-soaked wrap around her neck.

Recent and not-so-recent films had been a strong influence on the young skaters. I spotted several monsters, some of whom I didn't recognize, a colorful assortment of Star Wars figures, even a grotesque-looking mummy.

The band finished tuning up and began to play in earnest. Billie moved to the edge of the lake with his microphone and signaled to several girls who'd put on their skates and were picking their way onto the ice. They skated over to his broadcasting booth to offer their comments on the event.

"Terrif. Emerald Point should do this every year," they chorused.

A dozen adults, many in costume, took over the benches, tugged on their skates and followed the young people onto the ice. Jane and Alice had promised to call friends and urge them to come, and they'd apparently succeeded in talking a number of them into it, although I didn't see either Jane or Alice in the group.

As the crowd increased, the band pumped up the volume to an eardrum-shattering level. Josie and her boyfriend swirled by me, skating arm in arm. She pointed back up the hill. "My mother's coming with coffee and soft drinks," she called.

And sure enough, Kate and two of her helpers were trucking her collapsible booth down the hill and setting it up next to Billie Jorgensen's broadcasting station. A perfect combination as far as this crowd was concerned.

Despite the cold, everyone appeared to be having fun. Of course, there had to be a few jarring notes—a couple of falls, fortunately without serious injuries, a lovers' quarrel, marked by the female half of the couple flouncing off the ice, or more accurately, executing the best flounce she could manage on skates without losing her balance.

As I moved farther out on the lake, I noticed a dark figure I hadn't seen before skating fast around the perimeter of the marked-off area. He was swathed from head to toe in black and wore a spectacular devil's mask which looked like a real Mardi Gras headpiece. I didn't recognize him. Perhaps he was someone from another school, I thought, as I noticed how the kids kept their distance, even stepping back to let him through when he crowded into their territory. After a couple of turns around the enclosed space, he skated rapidly out onto the lake.

Not good, I thought as I watched him disappear from sight. What if one of the skaters was injured, or lost or ran into some kind of trouble out on the lake? We hadn't discussed possibilities like that. The agency which handled the town's insurance coverage would be ready to drop us flat if we were at fault.

I started to work my way toward the bank, but my progress was blocked by a girl wearing a doctor's white coat over her ski clothes and swinging a stethoscope while she guided a Frankenstein monster along. I found an open spot behind a couple who appeared to be vegetables, beets apparently, since they'd stuffed their red long johns and shirts to overflowing and topped them off with green knit watch caps with spouts of green crepe paper poking up at the top.

As I headed for Kate's stand, I realized it was starting to snow. The lights, which had been turned on along the shore, even those on the dock and boathouse, were already shrouded in a veil of white

When I turned back to survey the scene, I saw that some of the skaters had begun leaving the ice. Beyond the lighted area, an almost total darkness now blanketed the lake. Any signs of the moon or stars had been obliterated. The lights on the opposite shore had been reduced to a distant glimmer, barely visible. The boy band continued to play, but they were running out of pep. The volume dropped.

I reached Kate's stand and asked for a cup of coffee. "I'm thinking we ought to close things down soon. Do you agree?" I asked her.

"It's started to snow. That's going to make driving treacherous. How long is the skating supposed to go on?" Kate said.

"We thought until 10 or 11 o'clock originally, but now we probably shouldn't wait that long." I searched the crowd, hoping to find Jane and Alice and get an opinion from them.

"Are Pauline and Reggie here tonight? He always knows how to assess weather problems," Kate said.

"They've got rescue squad duty tonight. They said they couldn't be here."

"Well we don't want to send any business their way, that's for sure." Kate turned away to pour coffee for another group of skaters who'd come off the ice.

She was right, of course. I hesitated to make the decision to close down the skating by myself without talking with the committee, but we needed to do it, and do it soon. I asked one of the girls who'd taken off her skates to go up to the house and see if Jane and Alice were there. I pulled out my cell phone and gave her the number. "Ask Mrs. Kennison to call me," I said.

As I waited for her call, I noticed how fast everything seemed to be changing. The few houses looming up out of the snow on this side of the lake yawned dark and empty-looking, their lights barely visible. More of the skaters had left the ice. One of the boys had started a fire in an outdoor stone fireplace, and a half dozen people huddled around it, trying to get warm, but it was too small to provide much heat or light.

When I turned back toward Kate's stand, I saw her talking to a tall man all in black. A newcomer, I thought, but when I got closer, I realized to my astonishment it was Tim, wearing something which looked like a graduation gown and swinging a large, dark headpiece of some kind.

I thought it was time to move everyone off the ice, but I hesitated to do it unless I could find Jane and Alice and get their input. More and more of the young people were gathering around the benches, taking off their skates. The band took a break I could hear cars start up. I scanned the crowd for Josie and Tommy, but I couldn't find them. I spotted two of the committee members still left on the ice and picked my way toward them to ask their opinion about closing down the skating.

The dark figure in the devil's mask who'd skated out onto the lake earlier appeared again, now circling the perimeter of the area we'd marked off. Suddenly, he raced toward me, arms outstretched. I lunged to the side, twisting my body, narrowly avoiding a collision. I tried to think this was an accident, but he turned and came back toward me again.

"Watch out. Watch what you're doing." I spoke loud enough so that any of the remaining skaters could hear, but no one seemed to notice what he was doing.

The figure sped by me again with only inches to spare. I tripped, almost fell, but managed to right myself. I struggled toward shore, more shaken that I wanted to admit. My right leg cramped and buckled under me. I had trouble moving it.

Several skaters pushed past me, heading toward the bank, blocking me, not realizing I'd been hurt. I heard the man in the mask coming back. I turned, and he rushed me again, skating toward me at top speed. He was almost to me when he finally swerved away.

"What are you doing? Be careful." I yelled louder this time and jumped back. He'd come even closer, startled me even more. My foot hit a hummock of ice. My ankle twisted. Pain shot up my leg. I couldn't straighten my knee. I doubled over to avoid falling headlong on the ice.

I limped toward the bank, bent forward, barely able to put weight on my leg, anxious to reach the shore. The snow had started in earnest now, blanketing the cove. This wasn't one of the light dustings which, earlier in the winter, had turned our village into a sparkling wonderland. This storm was gathering force as if anxious to make up for its delayed arrival. The wind howled down the lake. The skies, dark and menacing, opened to deluge us with a fresh outpouring of snow.

I was moving even more slowly now, buffeted by the wind,

favoring my right leg. Up on the hill, I could see more skaters crowding around the benches. Some didn't even wait for a seat, but dropped to the ground to pull off their skates. People grabbed for their boots, then hurried to their cars. On the road, shadowy forms circled the parked cars, brushing off the snow.

Kate was dismantling her stand. I called her name, but I couldn't make her hear me. Two of the girls on the committee lifted the stand and, slipping and sliding, helped lug it up the hill to her van. Another followed with the few boxes of refreshments which were left.

The dark figure raced toward me again, forcing me back to the edge of the rink. Except now there was no edge to the rink. Someone on the committee had taken down the poles and ropes. The ice was open. I was forced back, closer to the large dock where the bubblers kept the water churning.

"Don't. The ice is soft here," I shouted.

But I finally acknowledged the truth. This wasn't some crazy teenager, a stranger to the lake, who didn't understand the danger around the docks. This maniac was not a kid. His actions were not accidental. This man—at least I thought it was a man—hidden behind an elaborate disguise, was trying to force me into the open water by the ice eaters. If he managed to do it, I'd have little chance of saving myself. I could easily sink under the ice and drown. I heard the bubbling of the open water. I was that close

I shouted again. "Stop. You're going to kill us both."

Suddenly, the lights along the shore went out. They disappeared all at once, as if snuffed out by an unseen hand. The lights in the windows of the cottages at the top of the hill, the street lamps which had been visible along the road, even the outlines of windows in the houses across the lake which had been no more than a dim glimmer marking the shoreline—every trace of illumination disappeared. The only light visible, the headlights and tail lights of the cars on the road, disappeared rapidly as people drove away. The sound of the bubblers, powered by electricity, stopped. Darkness, thick and silent, blanketed the lake.

The figure charged at me again. Even in the black void, I could make out the outline of his body and the shape of an arm held aloft. He was carrying something in his hand, a hockey stick maybe or a broom left behind after the broom ball game. Whatever it was, he lofted it high as he raced toward me.

He forced me back even closer to the dock. The ice felt soft under my feet. I sensed one skate start to break through, catching in the mushy surface as I tried to move it. I turned and lunged for where I thought the dock must be, but there was nothing there. I managed to right myself, struggled to make out a post, anything I could grab hold of which would keep me from plunging into the open water near the ice eaters. Dark shadows hid everything, disguised everything. I couldn't see the dock even though I knew it must be there. The bubblers stayed silent. There was no sound except the scrape of the man's skates as he came toward me.

"Help. Somebody help me," I shouted. I was wasting my breath. There was no one to help.

I had no weapon, nothing to protect myself with. I could think of only one thing to do, so I did it. I reached up and grabbed the strings of beads around my neck, the necklaces Josie had given me, the beads she'd promised would bring me good luck. I tugged hard with both hands, yanked on them with all the strength I could muster until I felt the strings break and I could rip them off my neck. The beads cascaded down, slipping off their strings. I lifted the bottom of my slicker and caught as many of them as I could. As the masked figure came at me again. I gathered up the beads in my hands and flung them onto the ice in front of him.

I couldn't see where the beads landed, but I could hear them clatter on the ice. The figure kept coming. My heart sank. I hadn't gotten them close enough to him to slow him.

A shout came from somewhere behind me on the bank. Even through the swirling snow, I could make out someone plummeting down the slope, careening wildly, slipping on the hill's icy surface as he stumbled toward the dock.

The masked figure saw him too. He cursed, the first sound he'd made, a high, frightening whine full of malevolence. He slammed the toe of one skate into the ice and changed direction. He lifted the hockey stick, veering toward the dock as he swung the stick at the shadowy form. He hit the beads then. I heard them skitter along the ice, then crunch under the blades of his skates. He stumbled, and began waving his arms around to try to steady himself.

He staggered closer to the dock, thrown off balance. I knew he'd be able to right himself in seconds, but I'd been given a chance, and I had to take it. I lunged at him, grabbed for the mask, got my fingers under it and tugged with all my strength. It didn't move. It fit tight on his head, too tight, but I didn't let go. I had to pull it off. I had to find out who this was. It was the only chance I had. As soon as he could regain his balance, he'd slam that stick into me, and if the blow didn't kill me or knock me out, the force of it would propel me into the open water.

He backed away from me, but I hung on. I could feel my left leg slip into water. The cold burned like fire, but I didn't let go. I pushed myself closer and felt him shrink farther away from me, dragging me after him.

Suddenly, I realized he wasn't shrinking away. He wasn't moving backwards in an effort to break my grip on the mask. He was sinking into the lake. He'd hit a patch of soft ice and his weight was too much for it. I heard other ice crack and shatter around him. It seemed to take forever, but slowly, more slowly than I would have thought possible, he slid down into the water, sinking into the lake and pulling me after him.

I yanked on the mask again, even harder this time, and shoved myself away, drawing on every ounce of strength I could muster. I felt water splash on my face as he struggled to grab hold of the ice. I heard pieces of it break off in his fingers.

This time the mask came loose in my hand, but I still couldn't make out the face. The figure, by then only an indistinct form in the darkness, flailed about in an effort to pull himself out of the water. I was lying close to the open water, too close. I knew the ice under me must be soft. I could feel water soak into my clothes. The cold burned like an open flame.

I wanted to stand up and run or at least get to my knees and crawl away, but I forced myself to lie flat, then inched myself along, trying to get away from the open space, desperate to pull my legs out of that freezing water. Miraculously I felt a dock post close to me. I seized hold of it, clung to it for dear life.

Suddenly, the lights came back on. As quickly as they'd gone off, they reappeared, gleaming through the falling snow. The bubblers gasped and started their rumbling

The figure who'd charged down the slope pounded onto the dock. He crouched down, wrapped one arm around the post and extended the other one to me.

I shrunk away from his outstretched hand."No. No. I can get out myself."

"Lorie, I can pull you out." Luke Prendergast bent over the end of the dock.

I thought I must be dreaming. Where had he come from? How had he ended up here?

"Lorie." This time he spoke with more urgency. He reached for my hand.

I took hold. The hand I grabbed was real, the skin coarse and rough as the edge of the dock. The grip was tight, and the hand lifted me up and slid me gently onto the dock. I lay back, exhausted, shaking with cold.

The figure who'd pursued me lay next to the dock without moving, his upper body on the ice, his legs in the open water, his face turned away. I still couldn't see who it was.

I tried to sit up, but I couldn't manage it. "Luke, we've got to get people down here to help us. Is anyone left up there?"

Luke raced back along the dock to the bottom of the hill, waving and shouting a great barking roar. A car parked on the road started up, backed around and pointed its headlights down the hill. Another did the same, then another.

Through the thick curtain of snow I could see people running toward us. Josie, half falling, stumbled onto the dock. "Lor, is that you? Are you hurt?'

Before I could answer, she was kneeling next to me, feeling my clothes. "Tommy, give me your jacket," she called back over her shoulder.

Without hesitating, Tommy peeled off the heavy parka he was wearing and handed it to her.

"Now close your eyes," she ordered him as she tugged off my skates, then my slacks and long johns. She felt my jacket and shirt, pronounced them dry enough to leave on and reached for his parka.

"Wait. We've got blankets here. Use this," someone said.

Two boys I recognized as high school classmates of Josie's handed her a blanket and she tucked it around me. Tommy shoved his arms back into his jacket, then knelt on the dock and helped the others lift the man who'd attacked me out of the icy water and onto the dock. I still couldn't see his face as they bent over him and began to pull off his wet clothes.

"Wait," I said. "Shouldn't we get somebody from the rescue squad up here?"

"They're both in it, Lor," Josie said. "They know what to do, and they've already called for an ambulance."

"Grab that other blanket. The first thing we've got to do is get him warmed up," one of them said.

I struggled to get to my feet, but I couldn't manage it. I reached for Josie's hand, and she pulled me into a sitting position. That was the best I could do. I leaned forward, trying to see my attacker's face.

I looked around for Luke, but I didn't see him. This was so much like what he done for me years before—helped me out of a tight spot and disappeared.

I sucked in my breath, steeled myself. At some time during that wild pursuit, I'd decided it had to be Ed Kennison who was trying to kill me. If someone wanted me out of the way, he had to be the number one choice. I'd asked too many questions, uncovered too many clues to his affair with Denise McNaughton, stuck my nose way too far into his business. I still didn't know if he was the one who'd killed Denise, but he'd probably get my vote.

"Help me up. I've got to get up," I said to Josie. I wrapped the blanket around my waist. She took hold of my hands and, with her supporting much of my weight, I struggled to my feet. I managed a couple of steps along the dock, even in my bare feet, but the rescue squad guys were still blocking my view of the figure lying there.

Josie leaned down to tap one of them on the shoulder. "Matt, lean back a minute. Let the Mayor see who that is."

I managed to take one more step forward before I looked down.

Jane Kennison's face, pale as death, stared up at me.

Chapter 20

I staggered back. My legs buckled under me, and I collapsed on the dock. Josie caught me as I went down.

"Is she still alive?" I asked Josie when I could speak.

"She is, but you better take it easy yourself, Lor. Don't try to talk yet."

That was exactly what I wanted to do—take it easy, not have to talk, not have to think about how Jane Kennison had tried to kill me. I leaned back against a post and let my eyes drift shut.

Maybe five minutes went by, maybe ten.

By the time I opened my eyes, it looked as if half the population of Emerald Point had flocked to the cove. Tim Donohue, apparently wanting to help Josie in any way he could, had joined the group on the dock. More of the rescue squad had arrived in an ambulance which was now parked up on the road. Jane, who was breathing but apparently unconscious, had been wrapped tightly in blankets and secured on a stretcher, ready to be transported to the hospital.

Two sheriff's deputies, Ray Reynolds and another man I didn't recognize, arrived and took charge. Ray asked for my account of what had happened—transpired was the word he used—and got names and statements from several people who'd witnessed Jane's attack on me. The other kept a close watch on Jane and accompanied her to the hospital in the ambulance

I looked around for Luke, but once again, he'd melted back into the night. I couldn't find him.

When Deputy Reynolds had cleared me to leave, Josie and Tommy helped me up the hill. Despite my protests, they steered me past my own car and into Tommy's. Josie ignored my pleas to go home and, with more care than I'd ever seen her take on previous drives with her, drove me to her house.

Tommy followed in my car. The roads were thick with snow, and Josie, new to this kind of driving, took extra time maneuvering my car into Kate's driveway. Tommy helped her get me into the house. Almost before I knew what was happening, Kate and Josie had escorted me upstairs and tucked me into bed. I didn't have the strength to argue. I was asleep in minutes.

Several times during the night I was half-awakened by the rumble of snow plows, but I was too groggy to take much notice. At seven o'clock, the radio next to Josie's bed kicked on to blast out a list of traffic advisories, church service cancellations and ongoing recaps about the storm's ferocity. The ski areas assured listeners they'd have trails groomed and parking lots cleared before noon. Essential businesses promised to open on a limited schedule. None of this seemed to pertain to me, so I went back to sleep.

A couple of hours later, I heard Kate tap on my door and call to me.

"Loren, can I come in? I've brought coffee. Investigator Thompson is on his way here to talk to you. I tried to stall him, but he wouldn't take no for an answer."

I struggled up in the bed, My knee protested along with several other parts of my body, but on my second attempt, I managed to sit up. "Sure. Come ahead."

Kate bumped the door open with her hip and set a tray down on the table next to the bed. She poured a cup of coffee and passed it to me. I spotted a plate covered with a crisp, white napkin, but coffee was what I needed first.

I drank half a cup of it before I could speak. "I was pretty out of it last night. When I finally came to this morning and realized Josie had given me her room, I didn't know what to think. Does this mean I'm close to death?"

Kate reached over and turned on the lamp on the night stand. "I almost thought so when she brought you in last night. You refused any medical care. I'm not sure how good an idea that was. You may still have to get an x-ray of your knee at some point."

I moved my leg carefully. My knee hurt, but not unbearably. "Maybe it will be all right. You say Jim is on his way here?"

"He said to feed you enough coffee so you could come up with a full report."

"I'm not sure exactly what that would be, but I suppose I'll have to give it my best shot."

The last thing I wanted was to drag myself out of bed, but after Kate brought me a second cup of coffee, I managed it. As soon as she saw I was getting up, she brought in clothes for me to wear and helped me into the shower. It took a while, but the hot water eased some of my stiffness and I was able to struggle downstairs.

I was sitting at the kitchen table, munching on a croissant when Jim arrived. Kate poured him a cup of coffee and took off fast.

"Mayor," he said. Cool, crisp, very professional. Not an auspicious beginning.

I jumped in fast. "I know. I know. You hate it when people try to murder me, but this time it wasn't my fault. I didn't even know who was behind that mask. My best guess was that it was the lady's husband. I was astonished when I saw her face."

"You thought it was Dr. Kennison chasing you around the ice? Why would you think that?"

"I asked questions."

"Meaning?"

"Okay. I made inquiries about the doctor's extramarital activities. A woman he'd had an affair with gave me some answers that put him in a bad light."

Jim waited.

I offered a few more details, avoiding as many names as I could. Finally I had no choice. I filled him in on most of what I'd learned.

"This all took place even before the carnival? And you were asking all these questions why?" he said.

"Because I never believed Luke Prendergast could have killed Denise McNaughton. He's a really gentle guy. Jim. He was a friend of my grandparents years ago, helped me out of a tight spot one time."

He gave me one of his disgusted looks—he could have gotten a patent on them they were that meaningful. "Didn't we have this conversation once before, Mayor? People don't come with any guarantees. I would have thought in your business you'd have learned that by now."

I hurried on. "Then I happened to run into a couple of hunters who confirmed they saw him up in the mountains at the time Denise was murdered."

"Happened to run into? What does that mean?"

"Just that. I tried, Jim, I tried hard, but they wouldn't agree to go in and talk to you about it."

He threw in another of those penetrating glances he was so good at. I skipped along quickly. I didn't want to name names, if I could avoid it.

"I thought it might be the doctor chasing me around the ice, that maybe he was the one who killed Denise. Maybe she'd threatened to tell about their affair, even though everyone said she was no hand to talk about her private life. I never suspected Jane."

"You didn't think it strange Jane didn't turn up for the skating? I thought she was a big wheel on your committee," Jim said.

"I did wonder why she and Alice didn't come down for the skating, but I blamed it on the weather. And even when she was chasing me around the ice, I had no idea it was her. I actually thought it had to be the doctor behind that mask. They're about the same height, and every time she came after me, all I could see was that headpiece."

I felt better. Confession is good for the soul.

Jim shook his head. "We have some evidence taken from the murder scene that seems to corroborate what you're saying. We've managed to keep it out of the papers, so far anyway. We were able to rule out Denise McNaughton's ex-husbands right away. The first one died several years ago. The other is in a nursing home in California."

I thought it better not to mention I'd found that out myself. A couple of phone calls had done the trick. No big, as Josie would say. But there was another aspect of the case I wanted to know more about. "The rumors about her male visitors? How much of that was true?"

"Took some time, but we've ruled out the ones we got names for. I get what you're really asking me, Mayor. We know that Jane Kennison killed her, but you're wondering about Tim Donohue, if he might be involved in some way."

That was exactly what I wanted to find out. "I know he was brought in for questioning. I saw him in handcuffs in one of your cars being hauled into the jail."

"You're right. He was brought in for questioning. He's a guy who seems to end up in suspicious circumstances on a regular basis."

I didn't dare say a word. Tim had been much too close to the scene of the crime. If Jim knew about that, he wasn't letting on—and I wasn't either.

"We have statements from a number of people who saw Mrs. Kennison chasing you around the ice last night," he continued, "but you can be sure she'll have a good lawyer, a string of them probably, and I don't suppose money will be any object."

His comment brought me up short. "Wait. Are you saying she might not be charged with Denise McNaughton's murder?"

"I think she'll be charged all right. But making the charge is one thing; getting it to stick is something else. Not sure we'll get a conviction."

I took a minute to think about what I was going to say. "Jim, where was Alice Simmons while Jane was chasing me around the ice? The two of them were always together. Then, after all the time they put in organizing the carnival, neither turned up for it. Jane was there of course, in that disguise, but where was Alice?"

"I think at that point Mrs. Simmons felt she'd had enough. We may get some help from her. She's lawyered up, but I think she's about decided to give us a statement."

Part of me wanted to let it go at that, but I couldn't do it. "What about Lucas Prendergast. Jim? I think he saw something at Denise's house at some point around the time she was killed. I'm not sure what. Any chance you can get a statement from him?"

"We can certainly try, but I wouldn't count on it. And even if we got one, I'm not sure he'd convince a jury that he knew what he was talking about."

So there were still loose ends to tie up. But fortunately, not by me.

After Jim had left, I found Kate in the living room. "You guys have been great. Josie was literally a lifesaver, but I want to go home."

"Let me call your plow guy and see if you can get in your driveway," Kate said.

"I'm sure he's been there. He sees a storm like this as nice money maker. He'll definitely be there twice, three times if I don't head him off."

"But you should eat something. Let me make you a sandwich to take home."

"Kate, I just ate two croissants. I'm fine."

I thanked her again for everything she'd done and left a string of thank you messages for Josie, still holed up in the spare bedroom, for coming to my aid on the dock, for bringing me to her house in spite of my protests, for giving up her bed. I'd be in that young woman's debt for months to come—and I knew it.

I drove home in a glistening winter wonderland. The snow had stopped and, as I turned down my street, the sun broke through the clouds for the first time that day to set trees and roofs, and even the lake itself on fire

My driveway was plowed. No problem there. As soon as I got in the house, I turned up the heat and made myself a cup of coffee. I settled down in my lounge chair with the afghan tucked around me and found an old Bette Davis movie on television. Ordinarily I loved feeling weepy over Bette's misfortunes, but somehow her troubles paled compared to my current problems with Don.

When he tapped on the door and came in around five o'clock, I'd put Bette's problems behind me. I was in the kitchen, taking a bowl of pea soup out of the microwave.

"Hi. Want some pea soup? There's plenty, and it's Kate's finest," I said.

He didn't answer me. He didn't glance at the bowl of soup I held out to him. He stood just inside the door in his navy parka and knit cap, staring at me as if he was searching for the words he wanted to say.

Finally he found them. "Loren, I don't think I can do this."

"You mean you can't eat? What's wrong? Don't you feel good?"

"I mean I can't live this way. I can't worry about you all the time."

I set the bowl down hard on the table. Some of the soup splashed onto the cloth, but I ignored it. I'd hoped I could hang on to my patience long enough to straighten out our present disagreement, but I could feel it slipping away. "All the time? I wasn't aware I worried you all the time."

"Maybe not all the time, but often. Much too often."

"You want me to promise something? Is that what you're getting at?"

"No. Not at all. I don't think it would do any good if you promised."

Fuel on the fire. "So, it's not only because I worry you. It's because I don't keep my promises."

"This particular one anyway. Even if you were to promise, and I don't see that happening, I don't think you'd keep that particular promise. And I don't want to live like this, Loren. I can't live like this."

I went on staring at him. I couldn't think of anything to say.

He swung around fast and banged out the door. He hadn't even taken off his coat and hat.

It was a long night.

The next day, I went to work.

Pauline arrived early, only a few minutes after I did. She thought I might need to go for an x-way. Even if I didn't, she wanted to make sure she got the agenda for next week's meeting typed up.

Jim telephoned to inquire about my knee and ask a couple of the same questions we'd covered in our conversation the day before.

Kate dropped off a special lunch basket she said was an extra from an order she'd done for a meeting that day.

Diane telephoned to say Mario was featuring a special lasagna dinner that night and suggested we go.

Josie cut her last two classes and stopped by to rehash Saturday's events.

No one mentioned Don's name, and I didn't either. I didn't have to tell anyone what had happened. News traveled fast in Emerald Point.

Cold Winter Nights is the fifth book in Anne White's Lake George Mystery Series. After the first, **An Affinity for Murder,** won a Malice Domestic Unpublished Writers Grant and a nomination as a Malice Best First Mystery in 2002, she continued the series with **Beneath The Surface** (2005), **Best Laid Plans** (2006) and **Secrets Dark and Deep** (2007).

Anne lives in Glens Falls, NY and is a member of Sisters in Crime, Mystery Writers of America, the Lake George Arts Project, the Adirondack Center for Writing, and the Lower Adirondack Regional Arts Council. She contributes to *Mystery Scene, Mystery Readers Journal* and local and regional publications. She makes appearances on blogs and BlogTalkRadio and will be starting her own blog soon.